Praise for Anna Durand's Books

"Anna Durand adroitly sets the stage for a fun romantic comedy. [...] Durand's two main characters are perfect foils for each other; both are conflicted and for good reason. Seeing as they try to make being roomies for two weeks work is priceless entertainment."
Jack Magnus, Readers' Favorite

" I loved the slow-burn, should we-shouldn't we, what's right, dilemma and desire that built and built until the steam had to escape. [*One Hot Chance*] is equal parts fun, steam, and moral quandary. [...] I am in love with Chance and his brothers already."
MaryLou Hoffman, Page Princess blog

"[*Lethal in a Kilt* is] full of hot sex, adventure, and so much laughter. I found myself laughing-out-loud at the antics of the Witches of Ballachulish (Logan's sisters) and the hilarious flirting and sexy banter between Serena and Logan. [...] Recommend highly! "
Sharon Clayton, The Eclectic Review

"[*Insatiable in a Kilt*] smokes from the very first pages... Durand's characters are a delight and seeing how they mix business with their increasing attraction for each other is entertaining indeed. [...] Durand's Hot Scots family saga just keeps on getting better."
Readers' Favorite

"I loved the Scottish in Ian and the strength of Rae, but the love of one little girl makes [*Notorious in a Kilt*] something to behold."
Coffee Time Romance

"*Gift-Wrapped in a Kilt* is a marvelous continuation of the author's MacTaggart family saga. Durand's story has an entertaining plot, and her steamy interludes are well-written...a celebration of healthy relationships between loving adults written in a tasteful and compelling manner."
Readers' Favorite

"I have enjoyed this whole series, but Emery and Rory [from *Scandalous in a Kilt*] have stolen my heart and are now my favorites!"
The Romance Reviews

Other Books by Anna Durand

One Hot Chance (Hot Brits, Book One)
One Hot Roomie (Hot Brits, Book Two)
One Hot Escape (Hot Brits, Book Four)
The Dixon Brothers Trilogy (Hot Brits, Books 1-3)
Natural Passion (Au Naturel Trilogy, Book One)
Natural Impulse (Au Naturel Trilogy, Book Two)
Natural Satisfaction (Au Naturel Trilogy, Book Three)
Dangerous in a Kilt (Hot Scots, Book One)
Wicked in a Kilt (Hot Scots, Book Two)
Scandalous in a Kilt (Hot Scots, Book Three)
The MacTaggart Brothers Trilogy (Hot Scots, Books 1-3)
Gift-Wrapped in a Kilt (Hot Scots, Book Four)
Notorious in a Kilt (Hot Scots, Book Five)
Insatiable in a Kilt (Hot Scots, Book Six)
Lethal in a Kilt (Hot Scots, Book Seven)
Irresistible in a Kilt (Hot Scots, Book Eight)
Fired Up (standalone romance)
The Mortal Falls (Undercover Elementals, Book One)
The Mortal Fires (Undercover Elementals, Book Two)
The Mortal Tempest (Undercover Elementals, Book Three)
The Janusite Trilogy (Undercover Elementals, Books 1-3)
Obsidian Hunger (Undercover Elementals, Book Four)
Willpower (Psychic Crossroads, Book One)
Intuition (Psychic Crossroads, Book Two)
Kinetic (Psychic Crossroads, Book Three)
Passion Never Dies: The Complete Reborn Series
Reborn to Die (Reborn, Part One)
Reborn to Burn (Reborn, Part Two)
Reborn to Avenge (Reborn, Part Three)
Reborn to Conquer (Reborn, Part Four)

One Hot CRUSH

Hot Brits, Book Three

ANNA DURAND

JACOBSVILLE BOOKS JB MARIETTA, OHIO`

ONE HOT CRUSH

Copyright © 2020 by Lisa A. Shiel
All rights reserved.

ISBN: 978-1-949406-32-0 (paperback)
ISBN: 978-1-949406-33-7 (audiobook)

Manufactured in the United States.

Jacobsville Books
www.JacobsvilleBooks.com

Publisher's Cataloging-in-Publication Data
provided by Five Rainbows Cataloging Services

Names: Durand, Anna.
Title: One hot crush / Anna Durand.
Description: Marietta, OH : Jacobsville Books, 2020. | Series: Hot Brits, bk. 3.
Identifiers: ISBN 978-1-949406-32-0 (paperback) | ISBN 978-1-949406-33-7 (audiobook)
Subjects: LCSH: Administrative assistants--Fiction. | Businessmen--Fiction. | British--Fiction. | New York (N.Y.)--Fiction. | Romance fiction. | BISAC: FICTION / Romance / Contemporary. | FICTION / Romance / Romantic Comedy. | FICTION / Romance / Workplace. | GSAFD: Love stories.
Classification: LCC PS3604.U724 O545 2020 (print) | LCC PS3604.U724 (ebook) | DDC 813/.6--dc23..

Chapter One

Rika

How can a man who designs sex toys for a living be so awkward around women? I work for the hottest guy on the planet, who has the hottest British accent on the planet, but I might as well be a robot sitting behind this desk for all the attention he gives me. Dane Dixon can barely look me in the eye, and as for conversation… Jeez, it's like watching a blind biker roaring down a curvy road on his Harley. You just know he's about to careen off the edge and go splat.

But damn, he's one sexy wreck.

This morning is no different. I'm waiting patiently at my desk for my boss to arrive—as his personal assistant, I make it a point to get here before him—when Dane walks out of the elevator and straight to my desk. Head down, he seems focused on the issue of *Forbes* magazine he's holding in one hand.

"Good morning, Miss Solberg," he says. When he glances at me for half a second, he swallows hard and resorts to staring at his magazine again. "Do I have any pointers—uh, I mean, appointments today?"

"Yes, Mr. Dixon. Today's agenda is already on your desk." Like it has been every day for the past twelve business days since I started working for him.

"Oh. Of course." He swallows again, his Adam's apple jumping. "Let me know when—if I, uh, have…calls or whatnot."

"I will." Rising from my chair, I tug my jacket down. "May I get you a cup of coffee, Mr. Dixon?"

"Yes. Thank you, Miss Solberg. One sugar, no cream."

He always tells me that, like I don't know how he likes his coffee after twelve business days with him.

Not once has he ever called me Rika. I told him he could, but he said it wasn't "professional." He also never smiles at me. I long to see his smile because I'm pretty sure it will be devastating. I'd love to hear him laugh too, but no, he never does that either.

Is he always like this with women?

Dane rakes a hand through his dirty-blond hair. The light glints on his glasses, so I can't see his eyes. But I know they're gorgeous. I got a good look at them on my first day here, when he'd taken his glasses off to clean them. He has deep-blue eyes that I'd love to gaze into for hours while his body is above mine and his hips are thrusting into me.

I haven't had sex in months. Working for a hot guy who ignores me is sure to drive me bonkers.

"Do I have a meeting with Celeste today?" Dane asks.

Wow, he got out a complete sentence with no "uhs" or "ums." I feel like I should mark this momentous day on my calendar.

He does seem kind of sweet, in an uptight way.

"Yes, sir," I tell him. "Ms. Arnaud is coming at ten."

He nods, head bowed. "Thank you."

Then he hurries into his office and shuts the door.

And I wonder again if he's like this with all women or just me. I've only seen him talking to men, so it will be interesting to find out how he interacts with Celeste Arnaud, the CEO of Bonsoir Beauty Inc., which owns Dane's company. He signed a deal with Bonsoir six months back, and now he's spending some time in New York at the company headquarters to prepare for the relaunch of his brand of sexual wellness devices.

That's about all I know. And I found that out from Celeste Arnaud's PA, who gave me the grand tour of the headquarters and dished about all the good gossip. Not that I like to gossip. But it's the only way I could find out anything about my new boss. My friends Elena and Arden know Dane, but they haven't said much about him. He has two brothers, but I didn't learn that fact from office gossip. I've met Dane's brothers, because they're married to Elena and Arden, though I hadn't met Dane himself until I started working here.

I trot down the hall to the break room and get two cups of coffee, one with cream and sugar for me and one with just sugar for him. After that, I hurry back to my desk, dropping my coffee off there. When I knock on the door to Dane's office, he invites me in, so I swing the door open and waltz up to his desk. As I set his cup down in front of him, he glances up at me.

For about a nanosecond.

"Thank you, Miss Solberg," he mutters.

And then he goes back to staring at the papers on his desk.

I've just sat down at my desk again when the phone rings. I answer with my standard professional greeting. "Dane Dixon's office. This is Rika Solberg speaking. How may I help you?"

"Hey, girlfriend, how's the new job going?"

I feel better already after hearing my friend's voice. Elena Linwood, now Elena Dixon, married my boss's older brother. Elena and I met a month before she hooked up with Chance Dixon, but we hadn't become good friends until after that. I'd missed their wedding because my appendix decided the day before the big day was a good time for it to explode. Elena had introduced me to Arden, who married Reese Dixon, but I missed that event too. A hurricane grounded all flights that time.

"Elena," I say, relaxing in my chair. "How's your hot husband? Are you wearing him out?"

"This is me you're talking to, not Arden. I give my hubby time to recover in between sex marathons. Poor Reese never gets a break."

Yeah, Arden is very...ardent. But Reese never seems exhausted to me.

"How's your hot boss?" Elena asks.

"Ignoring me. Does he always stammer?"

"Dane? No, he's well-spoken. You should've heard the pitch he gave Celeste when she was considering merging his company with Bonsoir. Chance and I listened to him rehearsing it, and Dane rocked his speech."

Which is the exact opposite of what I've experienced with him. God, it must be me. He thinks I'm repulsive or stupid or something.

"I'll take your word for that," I tell Elena. "Did you just call to chat? Because I am at work, you know."

"Yeah, I know. I called to ask if you want to have lunch with me and Arden on Thursday. She's flying in from England with Reese the evening before, so we're going on a shopping spree."

These ladies can out-shop anyone—including me, but that's not much of an accomplishment. I don't like shopping. Yeah, that makes me a freak of nature.

"Sure," I say, "I'd love to see you guys."

"Great. We girls really need to catch up." She hesitates, then asks, "Does Dane really stammer when he talks to you?"

"Oh yes. He stammers, he blushes, he avoids looking at me… You get the picture."

"Wow. He must like you a lot."

I hold the phone away from my face to stare at it for half a second, then I return it to my ear. "Are you nuts? He acts like he can't stand being around me."

Elena laughs. "Oh sweetie, that's not how Dane acts when he doesn't like someone. If he can't untie his tongue around you, then he definitely has a giant crush on you."

A crush? Oh please. A giant crush? Double oh please.

No one has ever had a crush on me, as far as I know, so I can't say for sure how men act when they feel that way. Men like me, sure, but there's been no crushing. And come on, Dane Dixon cannot like me that way.

What, am I twelve years old again? A crush. That's just plain silly.

I tell Elena that, and she laughs again.

"Time will tell," she says in a knowing tone. "This is Monday. When I see you on Thursday, I predict you will have changed your opinion about Dane Dixon."

"After more than two weeks with him, I rather doubt he's suddenly going to start acting smitten."

"We'll see." She switches to a whisper when she adds, "I'll get Chance to talk to Dane."

"About me? No way, Elena. Don't you dare do that."

"To be honest, Chance will probably do that anyway. He likes to keep tabs on his brothers."

"Does 'keeping tabs' mean meddling?"

"Um…probably."

I stifle a pathetic moan. "I have to get back to work. See you Thursday."

"Looking forward to it."

Elena and I hang up, and I go back to sorting through emails. Dane likes everything to be organized in subfolders so he can tell at a glance which messages are the most urgent. I'm in the middle of doing that when Celeste Arnaud walks out of the elevator into my little domain.

She stops at my desk. "Good morning, Rika darling. You look lovely today. Has Dane told you that?"

"No." I squirm a little, uncomfortable with her question after what Elena suggested concerning my boss. "It wouldn't be professional."

"Nonsense. Complimenting someone is not unethical."

I hike up my shoulders. "Mr. Dixon thinks a lot of things are unprofessional, unethical, un-whatever. Honestly, Ms. Arnaud, I don't think he likes me. Maybe you should get him a different PA."

She waves a hand to dismiss my claim. "He's anxious, that's all. Not used to the corporate lifestyle yet. And please, call me Celeste. I've told you before I don't stand on formality."

"Yes, I remember. Sorry, Celeste."

"That's all right." She glances at the closed door to Dane's office, then smirks at me. "Should I wait for you to announce me, like we're at King Henry's court?"

"No, but I will let him know you're here." I grab the phone off my desk and punch in the extension for Dane's office phone. When he picks up, I say, "Celeste Arnaud is here, Mr. Dixon."

"Please send her in. Thank you, Miss Solberg."

I hang up and motion toward the door. "He's ready for you."

Celeste leans in to pat my hand. "Don't worry, dear, I'll take care of Dane."

She strides into his office and shuts the door.

Take care of him? What on earth does that mean?

I have a feeling whatever she does will not put my boss in a good mood.

Chapter Two

Dane

Celeste Arnaud walks into my office like she owns it. Technically, she does. The woman is the billionaire CEO of Bonsoir Beauty Inc., and I am sitting in an office in the corporate headquarters. The chair I'm sitting in belongs to her. All my devices, my factory in England, and all my employees now belong to her ever since I signed a contract with Bonsoir. My arse probably belongs to her too.

Still, I like Celeste. It's hard not to like her. She may be in her seventies, but she loves to make racy jokes, and she loves to admire young men. Sometimes she licks her lips when she's looking at me, which makes me feel like a side of beef sizzling on a grill. Celeste is also the grandmother of my newest sister-in-law, Arden. That makes her family, in a way.

Celeste takes a seat on one of the chairs opposite my desk. She crosses her legs and leans back. "Dane darling, how are you? Looking scrumptious as ever, I see."

She calls everyone "darling." I've gotten used to it. I've also gotten used to being called "scrumptious" and "delicious" and "one hot beefcake."

"You're looking well too," I say.

Her blonde hair has grown a bit longer than when we'd first met, but it looks good on her. Despite her age, she stays trim and has no wrinkles—but Arden has informed everyone, in front of Celeste, that her grandmother keeps the best plastic surgeon in the world on retainer, in case she needs any touch-ups. Celeste doesn't care if her granddaughter says things like that. They are a strange family.

"Thank you," Celeste says. "Now, tell me why you're treating Rika so horribly that she thinks you hate her. Are you lusting after her? Is that the problem? I wouldn't blame you. She is beautiful and intelligent, so I'm sure you'd love to spend the night with Rika. Why don't you just do it?"

"What?" I stammer for a moment before I can give her a response that sounds anything like words. "Miss Solberg works for me. I can't do anything of the sort. Not that I want to."

"Aren't we friends, Dane?"

"Yes." What that has to do with anything, I have no idea.

"Then don't act so shocked when I bring up a sensitive subject. You know that's the way I am."

Oh yes, I know that. But she's never suggested anything like what she said a minute ago. It's insane. I cannot fuck Rika, even if I want to. Which I don't. I have no time for sex, much less romance, and Rika Solberg seems like the sort who needs more from a man.

Yes, I know that after speaking a grand total of thirty words to her.

"I don't have room in my life for a relationship," I say. "The re-launch is taking up all of my time."

"That's horse shit, and you know it." She slides forward in her chair until only her bottom rests on it. "Dane darling, your celibacy will ruin our re-launch. You need a girlfriend. If you want to date Rika, all you need to do is ask her and then report the relationship to HR if you decide to pursue one. Though it might be best if I reassigned her to someone else, to avoid any perception of an ethical dilemma."

I grab my coffee cup and down the last of its contents in one gulp. I drink too fast, which makes me cough. "What the bloody hell does my love life have to do with anything?"

"You sell sex," Celeste tells me in a tone that suggests I'm profoundly dense.

"No, I design sexual wellness devices."

She laughs softly, smiling at me with affection. "Women use your devices to give themselves orgasms. Do you think they want to know the man who designs the vibrators they use is holed up inside a tool shed in the woods, alone, like the Unabomber?" She tsks. "No, dear, they want to see a vibrant, sexy hunk of a man who has a bombshell on his arm."

"What are you talking about? No one is going to see me."

"Oh yes they are." She points a finger at me. "You are the face of the company. That's why we're re-branding it as Dane's Delights." She waves a hand like she's shooing away a fly. "The name you had for it was too boring."

"What's wrong with Bedroom Buddies?"

She snorts, clearly trying not to laugh at me. "It sounds like you're selling alarm clocks. Like it or not, Dane, we—*you* are selling sex. That means you need to embody the concept. A recluse who works twenty-four hours a day and lives on frozen dinners is not sexy."

I start to complain but shut my mouth before one syllable emerges. Maybe she's right. Maybe I do have a responsibility to seem less…reclusive. Celeste had told me from the beginning our partnership would require I make some changes, in my company and myself. I assumed she meant I would need to attend board meetings, not that she would instruct me to find a girlfriend.

But I signed the contract. I knew what I was getting into. Mostly.

"Fine," I say. "You pick someone, and I'll go out with her."

"I don't run a dating service." She tilts her head to the left. "Though maybe that should be the next addition to the Bonsoir ensemble. Well, at any rate, I cannot find you a girl. You need to do that yourself."

"How am I meant to meet a woman? You've got me scheduled for so many meetings I barely have time to drink my coffee."

"I know, darling, but you're a smart, capable man. You'll figure something out. And do it fast."

"How fast?"

"This week would be best. Honestly, it shouldn't be that hard for a gorgeous, charming man like you to meet a woman. She doesn't need to be the love of your life." Celeste stands up. "I have another meeting to get to."

"What?" I stand up too. "Was this meeting strictly a chance for you to order me to get a girlfriend?"

"Yes." She leans across the desk to pat my cheek. "See? I knew you were a smart boy. Oh, by the way, how are those two new devices coming along?"

"Very well." It's bollocks, but I can't tell her the truth. I haven't come up with a single good idea for a new device since the day Bonsoir swallowed up my company, and I've had no ideas at all since the day Celeste commanded me to design something new.

Celeste pats my cheek and leaves.

And I drop onto my chair again. Find a girlfriend? How the fuck am I meant to do that? I'm living in a strange city, for two months, and I don't know anyone here. My brother Chance lives in New Hampshire. My brother Reese alternates between New York and England, but he's over there until later this week. Besides, I can't ask my brothers for recommendations.

Chance, could you ask around for me? I need a woman, immediately. Doesn't matter if she likes me, just that she's pretty and willing to hang on my arm like a bloody ornament.

No, I'm not saying that.

Reese, you used to shag every woman in the UK. Could you loan me one of your ex-lovers?

That's even worse.

I have a week to find a girlfriend. Though I'm not as popular with women as my brothers used to be, I'm not completely incompetent. Even Celeste called me charming. Yet lately, I feel like I have no idea how to speak to a woman, much less convince one to date me. Working too much has left me…out of practice. It doesn't help that the last woman I took out on a date had wanted to go home with me only because she hoped I'd use my devices on her. She wasn't the first to want that, but she also seemed disappointed that I'm not "kinky."

In my mind, I hear the last words she said to me. *Why can't you be as exciting as your toys?*

A knock at the door alerts me to the fact Rika is about to enter my office. She's very polite, always knocking before entering and saying "please" and "thank you." Her politeness makes me want to bend her over my desk and do things an employer should not do.

I sit up taller, straighten my tie, and clear my throat. "Come in, Miss Solberg."

Rika sashays into my office.

Christ, she's beautiful. Long, chestnut hair that glistens in the sunlight coming through the windows. A perfect mouth, made scarlet red by the lipstick she wears. Those breasts, that arse, the way her hips sway when she walks. And the high heels she has on...

She walks up to my desk and offers me a folder. "Celeste wanted me to give you the latest projections for sales in the first month after the re-launch of Dane's Delights."

My name will be on every package that's sold. My name. Fuck, it's embarrassing. Do I really want women thinking of me and the word delight while they're using my devices?

I'd love to hear Rika Solberg whisper my name and the word delight in my ear. I'd love to watch her availing herself of my devices too. An image of that explodes in my mind, and blood rushes to my loins.

Rika always has that effect on me. She is the sexiest woman I've ever seen. For some reason, I can do nothing but stammer and splutter in her presence. I can't make myself look her in the eye either. She has the most beautiful eyes, pale brown with flecks of brilliant green. As soon as I think about her eyes, I can't stop myself from gazing into them.

I really should know better by now. Meeting her gaze makes my cock ache and my mouth spew nonsense.

"M-Miss Solberg," I say, sounding like a ruddy moron, "please—I mean, thank you. It—yes, I needed this."

I snatch the folder from her and pretend to be obsessed with its contents, though I have no idea what the papers inside it say. I expect her to leave.

She doesn't. Instead, she says, "Can I get you more coffee?"

"No. No, I—" *Shut up, you idiot.* But my mouth has other ideas. "I'm fine, thank you."

At least I managed a complete, if brief, sentence that made sense.

She still doesn't leave.

The woman smells like…I don't know. Something delicious. It reminds me of the sweets my mother used to make for us, but it smells even better wafting off Rika Solberg's body. Why does she smell that way? I've never heard of perfume scented like baked goods and candies. Is Rika trying to drive me insane? Maybe I should order her to wear loose-fitting clothes and some of those horrible sensible shoes. And I should tell her to stop brushing her hair. No more makeup either. Definitely no lipstick. And stop smelling so good too, please.

"Celeste told me to stay until you've gone over those numbers," Rika tells me. "Then I'm supposed to get you to sign off on it and send all of it back to her."

"Oh." I flip through the pages, not seeing a single number or letter that's printed on them, then I sign the last page and hand the folder back to Rika. "Here it is."

Her lips pucker just a little, and her brows tighten. "You looked at the numbers so fast. Are you sure you don't want to take more time?"

Not with her in the room. Watching me. Smelling so fucking good.

I wave her away, though she doesn't move. "It's fine. Thank you."

"Okay, if you're sure." She bites her lip, which makes me want to sink my teeth into every part of her body. "Is there anything else I can do for you?"

Those innocent words trigger something in me, like the switch that keeps me from saying insane things has been flipped, and my mouth wants me to sound like a lunatic. Celeste's command that I find a girlfriend replays in my mind.

And I have the worst idea. But it sounds like the best idea, like my only option, like the sort of thing I shouldn't do but want to do, badly—for reasons I can't explain. Rika is beautiful. And sexy. And clever. She would make the perfect ornament for my arm, when I'm forced to attend public events related to the re-launch. But I can't. She works for me.

I could fire her.

Yes, then she'll be thrilled to become my trophy girlfriend. *What a bloody moron you are.* If I phrase it differently, as if it's a business arrangement, then maybe it won't sound like such an insane idea.

"Are you okay?" Rika asks.

For once, my brain and my cock are in complete agreement. I meet her gaze. "Actually, there is one more thing you could do for me."

"What is it?"

The words "be my trophy girlfriend" get lodged in my throat. I open my mouth, but the only sound that comes out of it is a faint croaking noise.

Rika leans over my desk, peering into my eyes. "Are you sure you're okay? Should I call a doctor?"

"I'm all right. No need for a doctor."

"Okay." She keeps leaning over the desk, which makes her blouse fall away from her chest, giving me the barest glimpse of her cleavage. "What did you want to ask me?"

"Uh…" I tug at the collar of my shirt. "Would you have lunch with me? I need to discuss some business matters with you."

"Lunch?"

Why does she look so shocked? It's not that barmy for an employer to take his employee out for a working lunch. Maybe sharing a meal with her will calm this lust and help me decide whether Rika might be amenable to the trophy girlfriend idea.

Yes, that sounds like a reasonable plan.

"A business lunch," I say. "Nothing untoward about it. I'd like us to get to know each other a bit, strictly to improve our working relationship."

She straightens. "Okay, sure."

I stand up. "You should choose the restaurant. I don't know the area."

"Um, it's nine thirty," she says. "I guess you're still on UK time?"

"Oh. Yes, I suppose I am." No, I'm not, but at least that gives me an excuse for not realizing it's still morning. "You settle on a restaurant, and we'll take our lunch at one o'clock. All right?"

"Sounds good."

Rika sashays out of my office.

I admire her arse until she shuts the door behind her.

Christ, I'm in trouble.

Chapter Three

Rika

At precisely one o'clock, Dane walks out of his office and waves for me to follow him. We ride the elevator in silence, ride in a cab in silence, and enter the restaurant in silence. He settles a hand on my lower back as we walk inside and while the maître d' leads us to a table at the back of the restaurant. The curved booth is smokily lit and secluded.

Dane had asked the maître d' for a "private" table.

I don't think he meant this.

We slide into the booth, but Dane keeps an arm's length between us. The maître d' gives us menus and then leaves us here—alone, in our secluded, sexy booth.

No, it's not the booth that's sexy. It's the man sitting beside me.

A waitress arrives before we have a chance to say anything to each other. She sets down two glasses of water, then takes our orders and hurries away.

We're alone. Again. In a romantic little corner booth.

Dane fiddles with his shirt cuffs. "Well, I, ah—We should—" He clears his throat. "Tell me about yourself."

"What do you want to know?"

"Anything you'd care to tell me. For instance, do you have brothers or sisters?"

"I have a sister. She's a doctor, currently working in Lebanon with Doctors Without Borders." Yeah, she's amazing. My piddly job as a PA sounds shallow and worthless in comparison. Not that I'm jealous of her. I love my sister. "Maddie is two years older than me. She's an epidemiologist, out there saving lives every day."

"Do you get along?"

"Sure. We always have, though we're not as close as I am with my two best friends."

"You have best friends?"

"Yeah. Don't you?" Oh jeez, that sounded rude. "Sorry, I wasn't trying to be mean. It just came out that way. But since we're getting to know each other, maybe you'll tell me more about you too."

"Of course. And no, I don't have best friends. I have brothers, and we are close, but I don't know if we're best mate close."

"Chance and Reese think you are."

His brows hike up. "You know my brothers?"

"Sure. Elena and Arden are my best friends."

Dane stares at me, his face blank, for several seconds. Then he guzzles water from his glass. "You're friends with Elena and Arden. I did—Ah, I didn't know that."

Why does he seem disturbed by the idea? "If you're worried I'll gossip to them about what you say to me, I assure you I won't. A good PA respects her employer's privacy and the confidentiality of work-related information."

"I'm not worried about that. I was surprised, that's all." He takes another, more measured drink of water and studies me for a moment. "Do you know Celeste Arnaud, then?"

"Yes. She's the one who asked me to be your PA."

"Why would she do that?"

"Because I needed a job, and she thought you and I would be a perfect fit." I realize how that might sound and add, "In terms of work. A perfect fit as employer and employee."

"I see." He's still holding his water glass, but now he's gazing down into it like water is the most fascinating thing he's ever seen. "How long have you been a personal assistant?"

"Ever since I graduated from college. I have a degree in liberal arts, which means I studied lots of different things." I wait a couple seconds to see if he looks unimpressed, but Dane watches me with interest. "Snooty people think liberal arts is a nothing degree, but it's served me well. My education included everything from math and science to ancient history. Whatever my boss wants, no matter what their career is, I have some kind of knowledge that can be useful to them."

"You must be bored working with me. I haven't asked you to do anything except answer the phone and schedule my appointments."

"I'm not bored." Because lusting after him keeps me occupied during lulls in my work duties. The thought of a gorgeous man like Dane designing sex toys… That makes me even hotter for him. And it reminds me of something I've wanted to ask him since day one. "May I ask you a personal question?"

"Go on."

"Why sex toys?"

He jerks his head up. "What?"

"I mean, why did you decide to design sex toys? It's not a common career choice."

Dane taps his glass with one finger, his focus on the water inside it. "I, uh, couldn't decide what to do after university. My degree is in mechanical engineering, but the job I got after graduation was unbelievably dull. I couldn't imagine doing that for the rest of my life. I got a different job but still didn't feel inspired by my career. After trying two more positions, I thought I could do better if I started my own business. But I had no idea what that business should be."

I inch a little closer to him.

He sets his glass down but still avoids looking at me. "The girl I was dating at the time complained to me that none of the vibrators she bought gave her exactly what she wanted. I asked what she did want and, ah, she, um, told me in graphite—graphic detail."

Is he blushing? No, it must be the lighting.

Dane squirms, his mouth pinched. "Then she asked if I could make a vibrator for her, since I'm a mechanical engineer."

"And did you make one for her?"

He squirms again, and this time I'm sure he's blushing. "Yes. She… liked it. Things sort of mushroomed from there. Within three years, I had my own small factory near the chocolate-box village where I grew up. Online sales took off, especially after Chance's girlfriend started raving about my products on her website. She had a blog geared toward single women, and she often wrote about sex. I hadn't realized how popular her blog was until she recommended my devices to her fans."

"What made you decide to merge your company with Bonsoir?"

"Celeste convinced me it would be a smashing partnership. She also promised to make me an instant billionaire once the product line re-launches." He scratches the back of his neck, grimacing. "Not sure I want to be a billionaire. What would I do with all that money?"

"Buy a small country?"

He almost smiles, finally meeting my gaze. "Thank you for the suggestion, but I think I'll pass on that."

"Just think, you could be King Dane of Dixonlandia." It should Hotlandia, but saying so would be unprofessional. "Doesn't every man want his own harem of adoring concubines?"

Dane stares at me for several seconds, then his lips slide into a sexy grin and he chuckles.

Holy cow, he smiled at me. And I was right. He is devastating when he smiles. And that throaty laugh... It makes me tingle all over.

"I'll take your suggestion under advisement," he says. "I'm curious what your last PA job was."

"For two years, I worked for a city councilman in Rhode Island. It was a tiny town, but we still had a city council."

"Why did you leave that position?" He winces. "Sorry. Not my business, is it?"

I shrug. "Doesn't bother me. I quit because the jerk sexually harassed me. He asked me to go to a conference with him, but it turned out he only took me along so he could come to my room late at night and try to get his grubby hands all over me."

"That's awful. Did you call the police?"

"No, he didn't do anything criminal. He got handsy, and I slugged him."

Dane smiles again. "You can take care of yourself, can't you?"

"Yep. I took self-defense classes and karate lessons." I cross my arms under my breasts and give him a teasing smile. "So you better not mess with me."

"I wouldn't dare." He glances at my breasts, which I've inadvertently pushed up with my arms. "I hope you sued that bastard."

"No, I didn't."

"But Chance is a lawyer. Did you leave your job before Elena met him? I'm sure he would be happy to help."

"I quit way before I ever met Elena or Chance. But I don't want to sue anybody. I just wanted a better job with a nicer boss." I tap a finger on his chest. "And I got one."

He bows his head, clearing his throat. "I'm glad I'm better than a handsy councilman."

"You definitely are."

Dane lifts his head. "I don't remember seeing you at Chance and Elena's wedding, or at Reese and Arden's."

"My appendix ruptured on the day before Elena and Chance's wedding. I spent the weekend in the hospital." I cross my legs, which draws Dane's attention. I swear I'm not trying to lure him into looking at my legs. It was a total accident. "As for Arden and Reese's wedding, my flight to England got canceled at the last minute because of a hurricane. I'd been visiting my parents in Sweden, and I couldn't get another flight until the next day, which meant I arrived just in time for the last half hour of the reception. So yeah, I missed the weddings of both my best friends."

"I'm sorry."

"Not your fault." I shrug. "They showed me the videos, so it was almost like I was there. We weren't really close yet at that point, anyway. I hadn't known them very long. These days we're three peas in a pod."

Our food arrives, and we chat some more while we eat. Dane loosens up some and has an easier time talking to me. He tells me funny things his brothers have done—especially Reese, who seems to get into a lot of trouble. Since marrying Arden, he's settled down somewhat. Dane also tells me about the people who work in his factory back in England, how they're like family to him. I tell him the story of how Elena and I met. After the debacle with the handsy councilman, I'd taken a receptionist job at a dentist's office while I looked for another PA position. I wound up working one floor below Raisa Volkov & Associates, the law firm where Elena was a paralegal.

Dane stops stammering during our lunch together. He smiles when he talks about his family, and when I talk about mine.

He asks if I want dessert, but I say no.

"I'm too stuffed," I say, laying a hand over my belly.

"Elena and Arden didn't tell you, did they?"

"Tell me what?"

He almost smirks. "That to us Brits, getting stuffed means having sex."

"Really? Huh. I'll have to watch what I say to you, won't I? Might get myself fired for sexual harassment when I'm just telling you I'm too full to eat anymore."

He studies me, his blue eyes obscured by his glasses. "Rika is a lovely name, but I've never heard it before."

"It's short for Fredrika, which is Swedish. My dad is from Sweden. He moved to America for college and wound up staying because he fell in love with my mom, who's American."

"You said once they live in Sweden now. Where exactly?"

"Gothenburg, or Göteborg in Swedish. It's on the west coast. My dad got a job there five years ago."

Dane pays the bill with cash, leaving a very generous tip, and we head for the front of the restaurant. When I see the dimly lit hallway that leads to the restrooms, I tell Dane I need to make a pit stop, then I go to the ladies' room.

When I come out, Dane is standing in the hallway, leaning against the wall. When he sees me, he pushes away from the wall.

I stop in front of him. "Ready to go?"

"Not quite."

He grasps my arms and backs me up to the wall, pressing his body into me, bending his head to get closer to my face. "One thing first."

Dane's lips brush across mine, tempting me with the featherlight sensation, and his breaths tickle my skin. My lids flutter closed. The touch of his lips, the feel of his body, it all leaves me paralyzed in the best way. I flatten my palms on the wall while my fingers curl, scraping my nails over the surface. My breasts rub against his chest with every breath I struggle to take in, and my head grows light, my thoughts spiraling away from me. His entire body cages me to the wall while the bulge in his pants grows and stiffens, and an electrifying tingle of excitement shivers over my skin, raising goosebumps on my arms.

A breathy moan rushes out of me. My body softens, and I part my lips for him.

Dane pushes his tongue inside my mouth, sliding it around my tongue, the movements slow and sensual like he wants to taste every millimeter of my mouth. He grasps my hips, rocking his into me while he tugs my hips forward, making sure I feel every inch of his cock and the way it's hardening against me. He keeps kissing me in that intensely erotic way, so gentle and yet so powerful in his ability to set me on fire.

I'm burning inside, ablaze with the need for him to love my whole body the way he's loving my mouth.

This is wrong, isn't it? He's my boss. We shouldn't be doing this. But I don't care, because his lips feel so damn good, his tongue feels so damn good, and the hardness of his body and his erection pressing against me feels like heaven. I revel in the way he teases the roof of my mouth right before he wraps his tongue around mine. Oh God, he knows how to kiss.

My nipples go stiff, aching for his mouth on them.

Tunneling my fingers into his hair, I try to spread my legs for him, but my skirt prevents it. I whimper, partly from the way he's kissing me and partly because I want him inside me more than I've ever wanted a man before.

He pulls away so suddenly I stand there frozen, with my eyes shut, for a few seconds before I realize he's not kissing me anymore.

I blink several times.

"We should get back to the office," he says, sounding unaffected and looking at me like I'm his PA and we didn't just enjoy a steamy kiss in the hallway of a restaurant.

And we go back to the office.

Chapter Four

Dane

For the rest of the day, and for two days after that, I avoid Rika as much as possible. What did I do? Nothing. Yes, I'm deluding myself in the worst way, but I can't work with the woman unless I convince myself nothing happened. I didn't kiss her. I certainly didn't thrust my tongue into her mouth and paste my entire body to hers. That never happened.

Christ, she felt good, especially when her breasts were crushed against me.

No, she didn't feel good because I never did that.

I groan at my own stupidity. Do I actually believe I can erase what I did by pretending I'd never done it? Maybe not, but I can avoid Rika, thereby avoiding temptation too.

Except I can't avoid her. Whenever she buzzes my phone, and I pick up so she can tell me about whatever call or meeting I need to deal with, I hear her lovely voice. She always sounds cheerful—sexily cheerful. And I wind up stammering and mumbling stupid things to her. I also wind up with a throbbing cock.

Every time she knocks politely on my door, and I tell her to come in, she sashays up to my desk to give me whatever papers she's holding. It's usually something I need to review and sign. With her standing an arm's length away, I can't think well enough to read anything, so I pretend to consider the document even though I'm not seeing any of the words printed on the paper. Then I scrawl my signature and hand the document back to Rika, trying my damnedest not to glance at her.

I do it anyway, every time. My eyes have a mind of their own.

And of course, I'm left with an aching cock long after she leaves.

On the third day, Rika brings me a large brown envelope and sets it down on my desk right in front of me. Naturally, she knocked before entering my office. And naturally, she looks exquisite this morning, in a pale-blue business suit that has a form-fitting skirt. Her shapely figure leaves me speechless, again.

"Here you go," she says, her tone as bright as her smile. "Celeste sent over the mock-up of the new packaging. She wants your feedback on it."

"Oh." I pry open the metal brads that hold the envelope closed. "Think—Thank you, Miss Saltzburg. Ah, Solberg. Sorry. Thank you, Miss Solberg."

Every time I look at her, even obliquely, I get tongue-tied. It's ridiculous, but I seem to have no power to stop it. And every time I look at her, I remember my idea, the one that sounded brilliant a few days ago but now sounds like pure insanity. Still, the longer I gaze at her, the longer I admire her figure, the less insane that idea sounds.

We have the chemistry to pull off a fake relationship. My outrageous impulse to kiss her in the restaurant proved that.

No, I can't do it. She'll report me for sexual harassment, and I'll plead guilty.

Rika pivots on her high heels and walks out the door.

When she turns to close it, I hold up a hand. "Leave it open, please. I don't like being shut up in here by myself. At least with the door open, I sort of see you out there."

I freeze, realizing what I've said. Why the fuck did I tell her that? Now she'll think I'm a pathetic fool who can't handle being on my own.

She smiles—with sweetness, not pity. "Sure, I'll leave the door open. That'll make it easier for you to let me know when you need something. Just give me a holler."

Rika returns to her desk.

I can sort of see her there if I lean to the side and squint. But I do hear her voice when she answers the ringing phone. She has the loveliest voice I've ever heard.

And the softest lips I've ever kissed.

Focus, you idiot. Celeste Arnaud isn't paying you an enormous salary to daydream about Rika Solberg.

Right. Back to work.

I tip the large brown envelope up, letting the contents slide out onto my desk. It's a rectangle of red cardboard with the words Dane's Delights printed on it in gold lettering. But it's the picture in the upper left corner that shoots icy cold through my veins.

A picture of me. My face. Below that, I see my name, and apparently, my new title—"Dane Dixon, the man behind the O's."

"What the bloody hell?" I shout.

Rika sprints into my office. "What's wrong? Are you okay?"

"No, I am not bloody okay." I raise the cardboard mock-up so she can see it. "Why is my face on the ruddy box?"

She shrugs. "I'm guessing Celeste thought it needed a personal touch. Besides, you are the face of the company."

Yes, I am technically the CEO of my little corner of Celeste's corporate empire. She left me in charge, but clearly, it's in name only. I would never have approved packaging that has my face plastered all over it—and that declares I'm the man behind the O's. What the fuck is that?

Rika bites down on her upper lip, waiting for me to say something.

All I can manage is a string of spluttering nonsense that never quite manages to become words.

"What should I tell Celeste?" Rika asks. "She's waiting for your comments."

I take a deep breath and summon all the wits I can still find. The rest seem to have flown away. "Please tell her I don't want my face on the box, and I definitely do not want to be called 'the man behind the O's.' I am not an adult film star."

"Okay, I'll tell her."

"And please take…this away." I shove the mock-up at her. "One viewing was enough."

"Sure thing."

Rika takes the cardboard monstrosity and hurries out the door.

I try to focus on work. I'm meant to design two new devices, but after months of trying, I still can't come up with anything. Women have always been my inspiration, but I haven't had a date, much less a shag, in so long I can barely remember what a woman's naked body looks like.

Though I have fantasized about what Rika's naked body looks like.

After an hour of racking my brain, all I have to show for the effort is a pile of crumpled-up papers in the trash bin beside my desk. If I can't invent new sex toys, maybe I can at least meet another of Celeste's requirements.

I shouldn't do it. But I want to do it.

No, I don't *want* it. I *need* to do it. For the business. Not for my aching cock, but for my company.

Clearing my throat, I call out to Rika, "Miss Solberg, would you mind coming in here, please?"

She hustles into my office, halting in front of my desk. "What can I do for you, Mr. Dixon?"

"Please sit down." I gesture toward the chairs just behind her. "I need to discuss something with you."

Rika settles onto one of the chairs, shimmying her bum like she's finding the perfect position for it on the seat. Her arse looks fantastic in that skirt, and when she's sitting down, the fabric rides up enough to let me glimpse her knees. They're bloody fantastic too, and so are her smooth, sexy calves.

I stare at her legs like a brainless moron for so long that she finally speaks up.

"What did you need to discuss?" she asks.

"Oh. Yes. That." I pull my chair closer to the desk and spread my palms on it, then realize that must look odd, so I clasp my hands instead. And I clear my throat again. Twice. "The answer—the question, I mean—it, uh—"

Fuck. Why can't I speak when I'm in her presence?

In the restaurant the other day, we had a normal conversation. I need to channel the calmness I'd somehow marshaled on that day. Slow breaths. *Don't look at her legs.* Inhale calmly, exhale slowly. *Look her in the eye, idiot.*

After taking a few calming breaths, I meet her gaze. "Be my girlfriend."

She blinks once, in slow motion. Her mouth falls open. "Are you asking me out on a date?"

Wouldn't that be the worst attempt at asking a woman out? But I don't want a girlfriend, especially not one who makes me crave her so badly I can't think straight. Why did I tell her to be my girlfriend instead of asking if she'd mind doing me the favor?

"No, not a date," I tell her. "This would be a business arrangement. Celeste insists I must have a woman on my arm at public events. So it doesn't look like I'm a recluse living in a garden shed in the woods, or something to that effect."

"Yeah, that would be kind of creepy."

Does she think I'm creepy? I don't care. Maybe I do a little. No, I *don't* care.

She wiggles her bum again, then leans back in the chair. "You're not creepy at all, but the idea of some loner loser designing sex toys… That is kind of icky. I can see how it might not be good for sales."

I still don't understand why anyone needs to see my face or know my name, but Celeste is the expert. I've done reasonably well with my little company, but now she's about to launch it into the stratosphere like a rocket headed for Mars.

Do I want that? It seemed like a good idea when she suggested it. Today, I wish I'd never signed that contract.

"So, ah…" I fidget in my chair, though I'm positive the discomfort I feel has nothing to do with the seat. "Will you do it? Will you, um, serve as my, ah…"

"Pretend girlfriend?"

"Yes. That."

She studies me like she's considering the offer.

I fidget more. Or maybe I'm squirming. Or maybe there really is a nail poking through my seat straight into my arse.

Rika nods once and slaps her hands on her thighs. "Yes, I'll do it. What the heck? I don't have a boyfriend right now. Hanging out with a soon-to-be-billionaire could be fun."

How much fun will I be? I can barely speak a full sentence in her presence.

Before she can change her mind, I say, "Thank you, Miss Solberg. I will, of course, pay you for your time."

An entire sentence. No stammering. Miracles do happen.

"Pay me?" Her brows lift. "I already work for you."

A nervous laugh bursts out of me. "Oh, yes. Of course you do."

Rika crosses her legs, resting one hand on her raised knee. "Come to think of it, you're my boss. Isn't this a conflict of interest or an ethics violation or something?"

Bollocks. I don't want anyone to think she slept her way into this or any job. Though Celeste said she could reassign Rika if I decided to date her, there aren't any comparable positions available at Bonsoir. I checked yesterday. But I've gone too far to back out of it now, and I have no hope of finding anyone else who will take on the task of hanging on my arm, not in the timeframe Celeste gave me.

Another bloody brilliant idea occurs to me.

"I'll have to let you go," I say. "But I can find you another PA job. My brother Chance knows a lot of people in New York, so I'm sure he can help with that."

Her mouth opens, her eyes widen, and she makes a soft huffing sound. "Oh great. I get fired from the best-paying job I've ever had. How is that fair? I'd basically be doing you a favor while I get shafted."

"I'll make sure your new position pays the same or more than your current job. Chance and I will find you the perfect position." I haven't asked Chance if he'll help, and I may need to beg for it since I can't tell him why my PA needs a new job. Well, maybe I can tell him—just not the whole truth. "Since everyone will believe we're dating, they'll also understand why I need to find you a different position."

"Okay," she says slowly, like she's not quite sure about my plan. "I'm not an actress, you know. What if I can't pretend to adore you?"

"I'm sure you can." I adjust my tie, though it doesn't need adjusting, and squirm again. "We have, um, kissed. That should be all you might ever need to do in public."

Her lips tighten into a smirk. "You want me to shove my tongue in your mouth at publicity events? While you glue yourself to my body?"

I cough, splutter, and finally choke on my own saliva. Once I've stopped coughing, I tell her, "No, we won't need to do that. Simple kisses at the appropriate times will be the extent of it."

"And hanging on your arm. Looking pretty and gazing at you adoringly."

"You don't have to—I mean, it's not—" I take a breath and start over. "You don't need to adore me. Just behave like a normal woman who likes the man she's dating. That's all."

She nods. "I can pull that off, I guess."

"I'm sure you can."

Has she actually agreed to my plan? Why would she do that? It's an outrageous thing to ask of a woman.

"Are you sure," I ask, "that you really want to do this? I'll understand if it's too barmy for you to handle."

"Nope, I'm fine with it. Could be fun, going out to swanky places, eating outrageously expensive food." She twists her lips into a lopsided expression. "Except all I own is work clothes and casual stuff. Will I need to buy expensive dresses or whatever?"

"I will buy anything you need."

"Wow, thanks." She taps her chin, seeming like she's analyzing something. "So, I get free fancy clothes, free fancy food, and the company of a hot guy. Yeah, it might be taxing, but I can handle it." She hops up and offers me her hand. "It's a deal."

I slip my hand into hers for a brief handshake. Her palm is soft and warm. "Yes, it's a deal."

"Great."

We're actually doing this.

I drum my fingers on my chair's arms. What do I say now? Should I arrange our first "date"? Maybe I need to wait until Celeste has an event she wants me to attend. Celeste didn't spell out the details, but it seems to me that Rika and I should be seen in public before the re-launch. Otherwise, it might seem like a got a girlfriend strictly for that purpose.

Rika is smiling, and it seems almost playful. "Since I'm your fake girlfriend, do you want me to fake sleep with you? I can fake orgasms, no problem."

I choke on my own tongue this time. When I regain the ability to speak, I say, "That won't be necessary. We need to put on the pretense of a relationship only in public."

"Shouldn't people see me coming and going from your apartment? I mean, that's what a girlfriend would do. Right?"

Oh bollocks. She's right. I hadn't thought of that before.

"Uh, yes," I say. "I suppose you should do that. I'm staying at a hotel, though, not living in a flat. You don't need to stay the night. We can, ah, work out the demon—the details. Later. We can work it out later."

"Whatever you say."

"Thank you, Miss Solberg. I appreciate your cooperation."

She smiles and laughs, though it's soft and not derisive. "Don't you think you should start calling me Rika?"

Of course I should. Bollocks, bollocks, bollocks. Why couldn't I think of that either?

"Absolutely, I should. Thank you, Rika." Speaking her first name makes my cock twitch. Or maybe that happens because her hips and thighs are at my eye level, and I can't help staring at her body. "And you should call me Dane."

"Starting when?"

"Right now. We should have lunch together too, at a romantic restaurant."

"Ooh, sorry, I can't." She makes a pinched face. "I'm having lunch with Elena and Arden. Would you mind making our first fake date for dinner instead?"

"Yes, of course, dinner it is. I'll pick you up at eight. Uh, you'll need to give me the address."

"Sure thing." She rattles off her address while I write it down. "See you at eight, Dane."

Then she ambles out of my office.

Hearing her speak my name... Christ, I've got an erection now. Her swaying hips in that skirt, her sexy voice, that smile—and she said my name.

Can I survive fake dating her?

Chapter Five

Rika

Have I lost my mind? The evidence suggests that yes, I have. Why else would I agree to fake date my boss? I've lusted for Dane Dixon since the day I met him, despite the fact he gets tongue-tied around me. That's kind of cute, actually. When Dane gets flustered, I want to climb onto his lap and kiss his cheek. Then kiss other parts of him, starting with his lips. Since I've wanted him to pay more attention to me, our new arrangement feels like a dream come true.

So naturally, my reaction was to say, "Yes, please, sign me up! Woo-hoo!"

Maybe I didn't speak those precise words, but what I did say amounted to the same thing. I got so excited I wanted to fist-pump right in front of my uptight boss.

Until I realized he doesn't really want to date me. He wants to show me off in public, so everyone will think he has a girlfriend and he's not a creepy loner who beats off while watching internet porn in his tool shed. Okay, sure, I get that. It's an image thing. But why can't we legitimately date?

I should've asked him that. Shouldn't I? But no, I was distracted by my tummy fluttering and my heart fluttering because Dane Dixon was speaking to me. In complete sentences. Mostly.

How stupid am I?

Maybe it's not such a bad thing. I haven't had sex in months, and my last date ended with the guy suggesting I should stop being a "whore" for anyone who paid me to be their work slave. I don't see how working as a PA makes me a whore, but whatever. Even before that incident, I'd been having an insane amount of trouble finding a guy who's not a complete jerk or so wimpy that I have to order his meal for him.

Aren't there any real men out there anymore?

When I had lunch with Dane the other day, he hadn't needed me to order for him or tell him where to sit. He hadn't asked me to sign a legal waiver before he kissed me either. Yeah, one guy suggested that. Dane didn't. He backed me up to the wall and *kissed* me, like he meant it.

Oh, I loved that kiss.

Maybe that explains why I agreed to Dane's fake dating plan. One amazing kiss and I melted for him.

Now I'm sitting at my desk trying to figure out how I'll survive making like I'm his girlfriend for almost two months when I'm not his girlfriend. I'll have to pretend to be hot for him, pretend to adore him, pretend to love making out with him. Wait… I'm pretty sure we're not supposed to make out. Simple kisses for public consumption only, that's what he told me. Why hadn't I pointed out that we kissed way more than that when he took me out to lunch? No simple peck on the lips that time. He had made love to my mouth, and wow, I want more of that.

Sorry, you can't have that. Dane isn't your boyfriend.

Right. Not my boyfriend. I need to remember that. No thrusting my tongue into his mouth. No sucking on his earlobe. No fondling his hot body. Absolutely no unzipping his slacks so I can close my hand around his cock.

Oh God, I'm in so much trouble.

I manage to focus on work until noon, when I have to pick up the phone and tell Dane I'm leaving for my lunch break. Yeah, I could walk into his office and tell him. Bad idea. Considering the fantasies about him that I've endured ever since our little meeting earlier, I know I should not set foot in his office for a while. A long while. Like, days. Maybe months.

When he picks up his phone, I say, "Just wanted to let you know I'm off to lunch."

"Thank you for letting me know. Enjoy your lunch, Rika."

I love hearing him say my name. Love his voice, period. And his accent. I'd thought Elena and Arden were full of it when they told me a Dixon man's British accent will drive any red-blooded woman wild. Nope, they weren't lying. Dane's voice makes me so horny.

"Enjoy your lunch too," I say. "See you in an hour, Dane."

And I love saying his name almost as much as I love hearing him say mine. Dane. That one syllable makes me so horny too. Dane, Dane, Dane. Even thinking his name gets me hot.

Snap out of it, girl. He's not your boyfriend.

I stand up, roll my shoulders back, and head for the elevator.

Then I realize I forgot my purse. Jeez, I'm hopeless.

By the time I get to the bistro where Elena suggested we meet for lunch, I've gotten over the initial shock of what I agreed to do for Dane. Yes, I'm fine now. Away from his sexy presence, I feel much better. No lustful thoughts. I've kept my mind focused on the tasks I need to take care of after lunch. Now, as my two best friends and I sit down by the picture windows and browse our menus, all I think about is whether I want a club sandwich or an avocado chicken wrap.

"How are your hunky hubbies?" I ask absently while mulling my food choices. Do I want potato chips or salad as a side?

"Chance is great," Elena says. "He sends his love, and he asked me to tell you he's glad you're working with Dane now and he hopes your energy and enthusiasm will rub off on his brother."

Just like that, my thoughts swerve back to Dane. That kiss. His lips, his mouth, his voice, his—

"Reese says kind of the same thing," Arden tells me. "But he used the word uptight too."

Maybe Dane is kind of uptight, but he's also shown me his sensual side. Kissing me in the hallway of a restaurant? That doesn't seem uptight at all. I get the impression I make him nervous, though I can't figure out why. But when he pinned me to the wall with his entire body...

"Are you listening?" Arden asks.

"Uh, what?" Great. Now I sound like Dane whenever he speaks to me.

"She's not listening," Elena says. "Rika, why are you so distracted? The menu isn't that fascinating. Is something wrong?"

Dane Dixon is the reason I can't concentrate. I've had a giant crush on the man since the day we met, and now I'll be dating him. Kind of. Sort of. Not really. But there will be kissing, and I can't wait for that.

I groan, but only in my mind. Nobody needs to hear how sexually frustrated I am.

My two best friends are staring at me, waiting for me to explain my distracted state.

"Nothing's wrong," I say. "Lots to do at work, that's all. I have to help Dane get ready for the re-launch."

"Dane?" Elena says, lifting her brows. "I thought he insisted you call him Mr. Dixon."

Oh shit. How am I going to explain the fact that Dane now insists I call him by his first name? For that matter, how am I going to explain it when my friends see me going out on the town with Dane, like we're dating? I know one thing for certain. I cannot tell anyone I'm fake dating Dane. My friends will think I've lost my mind, which I probably have. Sure, they'd love it if I dated their brother-in-law for real, but that's not what he wants.

What choice do I have? None. So I tell them sort of the truth but leave out the part where it's all for show, not a real relationship.

"Dane and I are dating."

My friends grin.

"That's wonderful," Elena says. "I knew you'd like Dane. He's so sweet and sexy, smart too. You'll be perfect together."

"How fab is this?" Arden declares. "Soon you'll be our sister for real."

"I would be your sister-in-law, not your actual sister. But it's way too soon to talk about that. Honestly, we just started dating today. Dane's taking me to dinner tonight."

"Your first date?" Arden does some golf claps while grinning again. "This is amazing. Ooh, we have to help you pick out your dress for tonight."

"The emerald one," Elena suggests. "It brings out the green in her eyes."

Arden nods, her expression serious while she ponders what I

should wear for my fake date with my fake boyfriend. "That's a good choice. But which shoes? I say the strappy ones."

"Yes, definitely. Those black stilettos would go great with the dress."

I groan out loud this time. "Are you two done arranging my personal life? Maybe you want to tell me what to order at dinner or whether I should have dessert."

"No," Arden says, "that's up to you. But there is one super important decision you need to make before your date."

"What's that?" I instantly regret asking, because I have a squirmy feeling in my gut that warns me what she's about to say.

"Before you go out with Dane," she tells me, "you need to decide if you're going to sleep with him on the first date or wait awhile."

I have never gotten horizontal with a guy on the first date. My friends know this.

"That's right," Elena says. "Decide before you see him. I'm sure he'll be wearing a suit and he'll look good enough to eat. He is a Dixon after all. Hotness is in their DNA. I think they have a special gene that makes women go wild just from seeing them in a suit."

"I went wild for Reese when he was wearing jeans," Arden says.

Elena rolls her eyes. "You were a virgin when you met him, so we can't use your experience as a guide."

"You had sex with Chance five seconds after you met, so we can't use your experience as a guide either."

I've known Dane for a smidge more than two weeks, and though I've wanted to rip his clothes off, I haven't done it. Not yet.

"Can we talk about something else?" I ask. "I haven't even had my first date with Dane yet."

Arden leans forward, pinning her gaze to mine. "Maybe you should wait to sleep with him. Kiss him first to make sure you have chemistry."

Elena huffs. "Why wouldn't they have chemistry? They've worked together for a while now, which means they'd know if they aren't attracted to each other."

This conversation is making me crazy. Will they ever stop talking about my fake boyfriend? I'd hoped dropping that bombshell would be easy and we could go back to worrying about what to order. But no, I'm not that lucky.

"I've already kissed him," I blurt out. Why on earth did I say that? "Well, he kissed me. It was fine, so you don't need to argue about whether Dane and I have chemistry. Okay?"

"Just fine?" Arden says. "Ohhh, that's not good."

Elena nods. "Yeah, your first kiss should rock."

"Did he use too much tongue?" Arden asks me. "Or not enough? There's a delicate balance between—"

"Enough," I say. Maybe I bark that word. I've never gotten so annoyed by my friends before, but I need to change the subject pronto, before I really do go insane. "Dane is a fantastic kisser. End of discussion. There must be something else we can talk about."

"Sure, hon," Arden says.

"Well…" Elena fidgets, biting her lip. "I do have an announcement. Chance and I agreed I should tell you guys, and I've been dying to do that."

Thank goodness. A change of topic.

She smiles with her lips sealed, but it swiftly broadens into a brilliant expression of joy. "I'm pregnant."

Arden and I squeal.

The other customers in the bistro stare at us, but we don't care. One of us was bound to get knocked up sooner or later, and we love that it's Elena who reached that milestone first. She waited so long to find a good man who adores her. Now she's going to be a mom. I can't believe it, but I'm beyond happy for her and Chance.

Once we've calmed down, Elena glances at me and Arden. "I wonder who will be next to go the mom route."

"Not me," I announce a little too quickly. "I don't even have a boyfriend."

Two pairs of eyes veer to me.

Oh shit. I forgot I have a fake boyfriend.

"Well, uh," I stammer like Dane might. Maybe it's contagious. "I meant that Dane and I haven't even had our first date yet. He's not technically my boyfriend until after that, right?"

Oh yeah, I suck at lying.

But my friends seem to accept my explanation.

Elena smirks at Arden. "Guess that means you're next."

"Probably," Arden says in a thoughtful tone. "I mean, we have soooo much sex that it's bound to happen sooner rather than later."

For the rest of lunch, I manage to avoid talking about Dane Dixon.

But I think about him. A lot. Way more than a fake girlfriend should.

Yep. I am in so much trouble.

Chapter Six

Dane

I'm standing outside Rika's flat, fussing with my cuffs and my tie and the bouquet of roses I bought for her. Is that too much? We're not really dating. This is for show, but I felt like I should bring her something. Maybe chocolates would've been the safer choice. Are roses too romantic? Then again, we want everyone to believe we're a couple, so maybe I should've brought two dozen roses instead of one dozen.

After standing there for a minute or two, I realize I forgot to ring the doorbell.

"Bollocks," I mutter, and I punch the button.

I can't believe I actually suggested Rika should pretend to date me. The words came out of my mouth. She agreed, which left me thunderstruck. I hadn't needed to do much convincing either. Rika said yes almost immediately.

Why?

The door opens, revealing Rika.

I almost choke on my tongue again, because she looks stunning. Her green dress brings out the green flecks in her golden irises, and the way it hugs her torso and her hips accentuates her curves. Her shoes have very high, very slender heels and delicate straps that crisscross her feet, leaving her toes and most of her skin exposed. She's painted her toenails a pale shade of pink.

And her hair. She must have curled it or whatever women do to make their hair look sexy. Rika's long chestnut locks bounce around her face in loose waves and fall over her shoulders, mostly bared by her dress thanks to its thin straps. I want to bury my face in that hair and suck in a lungful of its scent. I know her hair is silky, because I felt it grazing my skin when I kissed her.

Her red lipstick makes me want to nibble on those lips, and her eye makeup has that sultry, smoky look.

Everything about her makes me want to fuck her right here in the hall.

Or we could go into her flat and have sex up against the door.

No, we can't. She's only pretending to want me.

"You look ravishing," I say, before I realize that sounds like a come-on. *Fake dating, remember?* Well, someone might overhear us, so I need to play the part. I thrust out the bouquet. "These are for you."

She accepts my gift and smiles, sniffing the roses. "Thank you, Dane. The flowers are beautiful, and they smell wonderful. Just let me put them in water."

Rika rushes off but returns a moment later without the flowers.

I offer her my arm. "Shall we go?"

"Yes." She slips her arm under mine. "Where are we going?"

"The Grand Salon at the Baccarat Hotel."

Her eyes widen. "Wow. I've heard that place is incredible."

"So have I, but I've never eaten there. So far, I've only ordered room service at the hotel where Celeste arranged for me to stay."

We start to walk down the hall, toward the elevator.

Rika curls her hand around my arm, leaning into me. "Where are you staying?"

"The Four Seasons."

She stops walking, swiveling her head to stare at me, her eyes wide again. "That's got to be the most expensive hotel in the city. Are you in one of those ultra-swanky suites? I bet you are. Celeste loves to go all out. She's a billionaire, so she can afford it."

I scratch my cheek, wincing. "I'm in the penthouse suite."

"Must be the biggest one they've got, right?"

"Uh, I don't know. It's something like forty-three hundred square feet." I glance around, trying to come up with a way to lessen the shock my accommodations have given her. "Your flat is very nice."

"You haven't seen it. So I guess you're telling me the door is very nice?"

She smiles teasingly and nudges me with her elbow.

"I, well—" No, I will not stammer through the whole bloody evening. Absolutely not. I take a breath to calm myself. "I meant the building is lovely."

"Celeste pays me very well, so I could afford to upgrade to a nicer apartment."

"Sorry, I'll make sure your new position pays the same amount or more."

"It's okay." She starts walking again, taking me along with her. "I agreed to be your fake girlfriend, so I can't complain about switching jobs. Besides, being your PA was only a temporary thing. You're here for two months, then we both move on."

The idea of moving on doesn't sound as appealing as it used to. I wonder why, but I decide to focus on our first date tonight and worry about everything else later.

Our first pretend date. I really need to keep that straight in my mind. She's hanging on my arm and smiling at me because I talked her into playing the role of my adoring girlfriend. That's all.

We make our way downstairs and outside, where I hail a taxi for us. Once we're in the vehicle, Rika hooks her arm under mine again, snuggling up to me, and rests her cheek on my shoulder.

She's playing the part, nothing more.

I know this, but I can't help feeling more...relaxed, with her warm body nestled against me this way. I want to nuzzle her hair, but that would be an idiotic thing to do. Then again, I'm supposed to be dating her—I want everyone else to believe that—so maybe I should shove my nose into her hair strictly to convince the driver that Rika and I are a couple. Never know, he might snap a picture of us with his mobile, and if we look like strangers sharing a taxi, that might ruin the sexy image Celeste insists I must have.

So I slip my arm around Rika.

But I stop short of burying my face in that silky, glistening hair.

"Have you been to this restaurant before?" I ask.

Rika lifts her head to give me a sardonic little smile. "Sure, I've been to one of the most expensive restaurants in New York. I date billionaires, you know."

She's teasing me, but I like it.

"Ah, sorry," I say. "That was a stupid question. I'm sure Celeste pays you very well, but not well enough to afford a place like the Grand Salon."

"Even if she did, I would've had to go there alone. My love life hasn't exactly been teeming with possibilities."

"No boyfriends?"

She shakes her head. "Not until you begged me to fake it with you."

"I didn't beg." I want to ask her why she said yes to my proposition, but her reasons aren't my business. "We'll share a new experience together, then, at the Grand Salon."

She lays her cheek on my shoulder again.

After our cab ride, we walk into the Baccarat Hotel arm in arm, with Rika smiling up at me like she honestly adores me. Has she taken acting lessons? I can't see any other way she could pull off a performance like this.

I had no idea what to expect from the Grand Salon, but I would never have expected this. The entire decor consists of platinum and off-white shades, but it's the proliferation of crystal that makes the interior jaw-dropping. It's everywhere, from the chandeliers to the glasses in which cocktails are served.

"Holy cow," Rika says as we're led to our table. "I heard this place was amazing, but this is just unbelievable."

I pull out her chair for her. "There's so much crystal."

"Of course there is." Rika says as if I shouldn't be surprised at all. "It's the Baccarat Hotel."

And now she sounds like she can't believe I don't know what that's supposed to mean.

"I remember the hotel's name," I say, and I might sound a touch snippy.

Once we've sat down at our table by the windows, she studies me for a moment. "You really don't know about Baccarat, do you?"

"Isn't that a card game?"

"Sure, but it's also the name of a famous French company that makes amazing crystal." She glances around the room, gesturing at the decor. "That's why this place is full of crystal. Baccarat owns the hotel."

"Oh. I see."

Why hadn't I known that? I asked Chance for a restaurant recommendation, and he told me he brought Elena here a week after he proposed to her, to celebrate in style. I hadn't researched the restaurant, but maybe I should have looked at the pictures on their website. Now I've made a fool of myself in front of Rika.

I clasp my hands on the table, trying not to act the way I feel—like I'm doing the exact opposite of impressing my date.

She reaches across the table to lay her hand over mine. "It's okay. I know about this place only because Elena told me. Chance brought her here after they got engaged."

"But I should have, uh, found out more before—Well, I should've known."

"Relax, Dane." She squeezes my hands. "I'm not judging you for your lack of knowledge about this restaurant."

Strangely, I do relax. The warmth and softness of her hands makes my muscles slacken, and the gentle tone of her voice soothes me.

"Let's see what's on the menu," Rika says, picking up hers. She opens the menu and raises her brows. "Oh. I knew this place was expensive, but I really had no idea. Chance must be richer than I realized." She glances up at me. "And you must be too."

"I'm not a millionaire. But yes, Celeste gave me a very generous salary and a signing bonus."

Rika's lips curve into a gentle smile. "Signing bonus, huh? I didn't get one of those. I thought Celeste was going to make you an instant billionaire, anyway."

"That's what she promised, once the brand re-launches. Still not sure I want that."

She considers me for a moment, but then goes back to perusing the menu.

A waiter arrives a few minutes later to take our order. He has a French accent, and I've never been good at understanding that. I stumble through ordering, though I have to ask the waiter to repeat things several times before I'm sure he got my order right. It's humiliating, especially since Rika places her order in French. I studied Italian at university, but I barely remember any of it.

I can't tell if the waiter is flirting with Rika, since I have no idea what they're saying to each other. He does smile at her, and they both laugh about something.

And I develop a sudden urge to tell that French wanker to sod off.

Rika asks me if I mind if she orders caviar as our appetizer. I shrug, and she speaks to the waiter in French again.

He takes our menus. "It's wonderful to see an elegant young couple who are so much in love."

The waiter leaves us.

So much in love? Where did he get that idea? I wonder again what Rika and the waiter discussed.

"You speak French," I announce. "Sorry. I didn't know you speak another language, so I'm surprised, that's all."

"I guess you don't speak anything other than English?"

"No. I've forgotten nearly all the Italian I learned at school."

She leans forward, lowering her voice to almost a whisper. "I told the waiter you're my hot British sugar daddy and you're trying to seduce me with a fancy dinner."

I've just taken a sip of water from the intricately carved glass, and I splutter. "What?"

Rika grins. "I'm kidding. I couldn't resist. You're so darn cute when you're flustered."

My mouth gapes, but I can't come up with a response to that. According to Reese's wife, Arden, being called "cute" is a compliment. It means a woman likes you. But Rika can't like me in the way Arden meant. Not when I behave like a cartoon character.

Our appetizer arrives, and while the waiter sets it down on the table, Rika rubs her hands together like she can't wait to devour it. "I've never had caviar before."

"Never?" I tap my fingernail on my crystal water glass. "I have. Caviar is…not my favorite food."

"Why didn't you tell me? We could've ordered something else."

"You seemed excited about trying it."

Her lips curl up at the corners, not quite a smile but definitely an expression of…what? Affection? I can't decide if I want her to feel affectionate toward me.

"You really are adorable," she says. "And such a sweetheart."

"Uh… Thank you."

I watch while Rika samples the caviar. First, her nose wrinkles. Then, as she chews and swallows it, her face lights up. "You know, that's not as gross as I thought it might be. Not my favorite food either, but it's not half bad. My family goes for simpler stuff, like T-bone steaks and twice-baked potatoes."

"That's much better than caviar. Do you get along with your parents?"

"Sure. We get together for the holidays, birthdays, whatever, and we always have a good time." She consumes another mouthful of caviar before she asks me, "What about your parents? Elena and Arden make it sound like the Dixons are the perfect family. I know Chance and Reese, but I've never met your mom and dad."

"We all get on well and rarely argue. Not much to say, really. We're boring."

"You're not boring at all."

I freeze with my glass a millimeter from my lips. She doesn't think I'm boring.

The waiter brings our entrees, and we stick to discussing the food and the decor while we eat. Afterward, I try to pay the bill.

Rika stops me with a hand on my arm. She leans in to whisper in my ear. "I should pay half. This is a fake date, after all. I'll give you my part once we're back at my apartment, so nobody sees us splitting the bill. I mean, I know it's common these days for couples to go dutch, but I figured that might embarrass you."

She cares if I'm embarrassed. She said I'm not boring, I'm cute, and I'm a sweetheart. Maybe I shouldn't read too much into her behavior or her words. If she were attracted to me, she would've told me. Wouldn't she? Or am I meant to take the first step?

Not that I want to or plan to.

I pat her arm and whisper to her, "Don't worry about the bill. Our phony relationship was my idea, so I will pay."

"Okay. Thank you, Dane."

"You're welcome, Rika." I love saying her name. It rolls off my tongue in the most satisfying way. "I am about to be a billionaire, after all. I can afford to spoil my not-girlfriend."

"You are such a gentleman. It's refreshing."

After I pay the bill, we take a taxi back to her apartment building. I walk her to her door, the way a gentleman would. Not because she called me that, but because I want to do it. I always walk a woman to her door. It's the polite thing to do.

Rika unlocks the door, swinging it open, but lingers on the threshold. "Thank you for a lovely evening, Dane."

I kiss her cheek.

She raises her brows. "That's all I get? I mean, we want everyone to believe we're hot for each other. Don't you think you should give me a real kiss?"

"Well—It's—" I want to do that, but considering how our first kiss affected me, I don't think it's a good idea. "I never kiss a woman on the mouth on the first date."

"Make an exception. For the sake of appearances."

"There's no one else around."

"But this building has security cameras on every floor. What if someone leaks a video of you not kissing me?" Her smile is teasing and sexy as hell. "Don't want potential customers to think you don't know how to please a woman."

"Ah…" I can't stop staring at her red lips. She might have a point about appearances. Or maybe I'm so desperate to kiss her again that I'll take any excuse. "Yes, you may be right."

I move closer, bending my head to seal my lips over hers. The first touch fires an electric jolt of lust through me, from my mouth straight down to cock. The scent of her overpowers my senses, and I thrust a hand into her hair, spreading my palm up from her nape so I can tip her head back. A breath rushes out of her. For this one moment, I let myself forget she's only pretending, that this isn't real, and I lose myself in the kiss. Her lips feel soft and slick and warm, and when I push my tongue between them, she opens her mouth more.

I can't hold back, not when she moans and grasps my arms like she wants to do so much more than kiss. Thrusting deep, I devour her mouth and gorge myself on the flavor of her, on the sensation of our tongues twining and our lips colliding while we both cling to each other like we need our bodies melded but the air between us has become an impenetrable barrier. Any thoughts I might've had left in my brain fly away, leaving nothing except the blind, overpowering hunger to consume this woman like I've never done with anyone else.

She grasps my lapels and drags me into her body.

All of her, crashing into all of me… It feels incredible. I back her up to the doorjamb and grind myself against her, heedless of the fact I have a raging erection that's now jammed into her belly. She moans again, the sound so erotic it's fraying my last thread of willpower. I grip her arse with both hands, kneading her cheeks, then whisk one hand up to her breast and close my fingers around it, loving the way her flesh yields to me—except for the stiff peak. I want my mouth on that nipple. Now.

But I don't do it. I massage her breast and her arse, knowing that's as far as I should go, as far as I can go. I shouldn't even be doing that. How long we kiss, I have no idea. It feels like an eternity of pleasure. I don't want to stop, but I have to break away and give up the feel of her body and the taste of her mouth. It's what our arrangement requires.

So I step back, creating a distance between us. "Good night, Rika."

My voice sounds rough, almost hoarse.

Before she can speak, I spin away from her and stalk down the hall.

Chapter Seven

Rika

I toss and turn all night, tormented by dreams of Dane kissing me, Dane's body pressed against me, Dane's hungry groans, the way he'd fondled my ass and my breast. Yeah, sure, I had hauled him into me. I can't blame Dane for how hot our kiss got, because I suggested a real kiss, I pulled him closer, and I ravaged his mouth like a sex-starved lunatic. Sure, I haven't had sex in a while, but sheesh. I should have more self-control, shouldn't I?

Not with Dane Dixon.

The man can barely speak to me during office hours, but on our date, he didn't stammer the way he usually does. He was courteous, respectful, sweet, and funny—and he even held doors for me and pulled my chair out for me. He behaved like the perfect boyfriend. But he's not my boyfriend. I want him to be. Last night I'd realized that. I should tell him how I feel, but he's made it pretty clear he wants nothing to do with actual dating.

The next morning, I walk into the office with dark circles under my eyes that no amount of makeup can cover up. Twice overnight I'd woken from a dream of Dane so turned on that I had to relieve my lust the solo way. My hair is still damp because my stupid hair dryer decided to break this morning, so not only do I look like I broke out the booze and had a massive bender after Dane said good night to me, but I also look like a drowned puppy.

At least my clothes and makeup look okay.

I've just sat down at my desk when the phone rings. It's Dane's extension.

"Hi, boss," I say, feigning a cheerfulness I don't feel this morning. "What can I do for you?"

"Come into my office, please. I need to speak to you."

"Sure thing."

I march into his office, and when he waves for me to sit down, I settle onto a chair across the desk from him.

Dane shuffles papers on his desk, head down, moving only his eyes to glance up at me repeatedly. He must notice my wet hair and my dark circles.

I clear my throat. "I'm so sorry about the way I look this morning. I know it's unprofessional to have wet hair at work, but my hair dryer broke and—"

He raises a hand to silence my babbling. "I don't care about any of that. Chance and I have found you another position."

"Already?"

It's been one day since he asked me to be his fake girlfriend. He already got me another job? Maybe the slutty way I'd dragged him into me last night has embarrassed him, so he quick found me a new job. Right. He got up at two a.m. to hunt for another PA position for me.

Well, with this guy, who knows?

Dane fiddles with his tie. "Yesterday, after our discussion about the...uh...fake orgasm—" He blushes. Really blushes. And he clearly remembers my joke about orgasms. "I meant the fat—the fake girlfriend issue. You aren't fat. N-not at, um, all. Or ever. Or—"

"Relax, Dane, it's okay. I know what you were trying to say." Jeez, he's even more nervous than every other time we've spoken. So I give him what I hope looks like a sympathetic smile. "This is all kind of weird for me too."

"Is it?"

"Yep. Take a breath and start over. This is business, right? There's no reason to be nervous."

He takes a breath and sets his palms on the desktop. "Chance has a mate who owns a home business, and he needs a personal assistant. His name is Eddie Masters. He films fitness videos that he sells on his website, and he also offers live classes over the internet."

"I love streaming exercise classes. It's more fun than doing it by myself in my living room, and I've never liked going to the gym."

"Neither have I." He picks up a sheet of paper and hands it to me. "These are the details about the job. You're to report there immediately."

"This morning?" I lean forward to take the paper, but an icy chill has washed over me. "I thought it would take longer to get a new job. This is so sudden."

"Yes, I know. I'm sorry, but considering our new relationship—" He freezes for a second, not even blinking, then clears his throat and adjusts his glasses. "I meant considering the business relationship we have. The dating business." He squeezes his eyes shut and hisses, "Bollocks."

I can't help smiling at his frustration. Every time he stammers or says the wrong thing, I want to hug him. "Take it easy, Dane. I know our dating thing is only a business arrangement. And it makes sense to get me a new position right away."

But the thought of not seeing him every day makes me a little queasy.

Which is so incredibly dumb. I've known him for a few weeks, but we hadn't spoken much until this week. I loved our lunch the other day and the kiss that came after it. I loved our dinner last night and the super-hot kiss we enjoyed when he walked me to my door. And that's one of so many things Dane does that no other guy would bother with these days. Walking me to my door. Picking me up at my door. Giving me flowers.

I read the laser-printed text on the paper Dane gave me. It's a printout of an email from Chance that outlines the details of my new job.

"Stamford, Connecticut?" I say. "That's, like, forty-five minutes away."

Or so I've heard, but then, I've never taken a train or driven a car from New York to Stamford.

"If it's too far for you to drive every day," he says, "I'll pay for you to rent a flat in Stamford."

"But being your fake girlfriend is my job too. How are we going to date when I'm way over there in Connecticut?"

"There are trains to and from the city. I checked." He offers me another piece of paper. "This is the train schedule for all the lines that go from New York to Stamford."

"Oh. Thanks." The way he seems so eager to get rid of me makes me feel like I'm shrinking into an ant-size version of myself. "I'm sorry if I embarrassed you last night. With that kiss."

And the way I forced you to plaster yourself to me.

He pushes his glasses up with one finger. "I wasn't embarrassed."

I believe him, which leads to one inescapable conclusion. He'd taken off so fast after our kiss because he'd been as turned on as I was. I'd felt his erection. His big, hard erection.

"Good," I say. "Thank you for finding me another job. This one sounds like fun."

"Chance told me Eddie is a decent bloke who will treat you with respect, not like that arse who harassed you at your previous job."

"Yeah, I don't think anyone else would act the way that jerk did."

Dane glances at the open door to the office. "Maybe we should say goodbye the way, uh, couples do."

I glance over my shoulder and suddenly get why he's suggesting that. A man has walked up to my desk—my former desk—and is sitting down in the chair I once occupied.

"That's your replacement," Dane says. "Not that anyone can really replace you. My new PA is here for a temporary position, with the potential to make it permanent later."

He's already replaced me. I know he had to do it, but still…I'm feeling queasy again.

Dane comes around the desk to me.

I get up too.

He pulls me into his arms and fuses his mouth to mine. It's not a steamy kiss. Our lips meet, and we hold our mouths like that for a moment without deepening the kiss. It feels wonderful anyway. I love having his body crushed to mine, so I can experience every single one of his muscles.

Dane lets go of me but doesn't back away. "Good luck at your new job."

"Thanks."

I let him take my hand and lead me out into the reception area. He introduces me to his new PA, Noah Smolak. The guy looks fresh out of college, dressed in khaki pants and a polo shirt. Did no one tell him how to dress for a big-time job like this one? When Dane gives the kid an assessing look, Noah cringes the tiniest bit.

"Good morning, Mr. Dixon, sir," Noah says, his spine ramrod straight. He even raises his hand like he might salute Dane, but he lowers it quickly. "Sorry about my clothes. I didn't have time to go buy a suit before work this morning. I only had two hours' notice."

Wow, this replacing-me thing really is a rush job.

"It's all right," Dane tells Noah. "I know this was last minute."

Dane kisses my cheek and wishes me a good day, then strides back into his office and shuts the door.

I hustle to the train station.

At least my hair will be dry by the time I meet Eddie Masters.

The train ride gives me time to collect myself. Walking into the office to find out I'm not wanted there anymore was like getting slapped in the face with a big wet towel. Dane still wants to date me, for show, but he doesn't want me around at work. I knew this would happen, but I didn't think he'd leap on the task of getting rid of me with so much enthusiasm.

The second I step off the train at Stamford, my phone rings.

"Are you there yet?" Dane asks when I answer the call.

"Yes, I'm in Stamford. But I haven't gotten to Eddie Masters' place yet."

"I forgot to mention Eddie is sending a car for you. The driver will have a sign with your name on it."

Glancing around, I spot a man holding a cardboard sign with my name scrawled on it in big red letters. I wave to the driver, who nods. "I see him. How's it going with Noah?"

"He keeps calling me 'Mr. Dixon, sir.' It's odd."

"At least he's being polite." I follow the driver toward a silver Lexus sedan and climb into the backseat. "I doubt you'd like it if he called you 'dude.' Noah seems nice. I'm sure you two will get along."

"Not as well as I got on with you."

I get a warm feeling all over when he says that. "You should take Noah to lunch. Make him feel welcome. The poor kid took the job with two hours' notice."

"All right. I'll take him to lunch." Dane lowers his voice to a husky rumble. "But I absolutely will not be kissing him in the hallway."

I smile with my lips sealed, holding my fingers to my mouth until the urge to laugh subsides. "Just buy him lunch like the good boss I know you are."

"Yes, I will." He pauses, like he's thinking about what he wants to say next. "I'd like to have dinner with you again tonight. For extra practice. The publicity campaign starts in earnest in ten days."

"Guess we'd better get practiced up, then." Practice making out with Dane. Oh, that sounds like exactly what I'll need after a long day of working for a fitness trainer and taking the train back and forth to New York. But there's a problem. I'm already tired from not sleeping well last night. "Um, I think I'll be wiped out after my first day at a new job, plus the commute."

"I'll order takeaway and bring it to your flat. It would be, ah, good for us to get it on—Uh, get in the habit of, you know, doing things together."

The Lexus is pulling into the driveway of a large house.

"Okay," I tell Dane, "we can meet at my place. Not sure what time I'll be home."

"Call me when you get off the train."

"It's a date." I decide I really ought to go all in on playing the part of Dane Dixon's love interest, so I add, "See you tonight, honey. Can't wait to snuggle with you."

Dane sputters, and I bet there's spittle flying. "Y-yes. God—Goodbye."

Click. Call ended.

The driver opens my door for me. Wow, another gentleman in the modern world. Of course, this guy gets paid to be polite to his passengers. I walk up concrete steps to the front door of a big, beautiful stone house that must have cost a fortune.

Seconds tick by after I hit the buzzer, then the door swings open. And I get my first look at my new boss.

The guy works out for a living, so I shouldn't be surprised by his ripped physique. But damn, he knows how to flaunt it. Eddie wears skintight blue shorts and a gray tank top, showing off his bulging biceps. His eyes are the color of coffee, his lips are thick and wide, and his face is angular. All of that gives him a ruggedly sexy look.

I should be hot for this guy, but all I can think about is Dane. What does he look like in workout clothes? Or buck naked?

"You must be Rika Solberg," my new boss says. While we shake hands, he keeps talking. "I'm Eddie Masters. So glad to have you here. I've needed a PA for a while, but it's hard to find someone who knows what they're doing. If Chance Dixon recommends you, I know you'll be top-notch."

"Thank you. You're very kind."

Eddie moves aside, gesturing for me to enter his house.

It's gorgeous, but I have trouble focusing on the interior design or on his explanations of the architecture. My mind keeps wandering back to my former boss, the one who kisses me like he means it, like he's not pretending, like we're dating for real. But we're not.

Maybe tonight, he'll change his mind about that.

I won't hold my breath.

Chapter Eight

Dane

I shouldn't have pushed Rika to let me go to her flat to-night. We could've waited until tomorrow for our next date, but I had an overpowering urge to see her. Knowing she's out there in Connecticut all day, every day, from now on... It makes me uncomfortable. I've gotten used to being welcomed by her smile and her cheerful greetings every morning. From this day forward, I'll hear "good morning, Mr. Dixon, sir" instead of Rika's lovely voice.

Why does Noah insist on calling me "Mr. Dixon, sir"? It's overkill. Either "Mr. Dixon" or "sir" would be more than enough deference, but he stacks on layers of it. Noah seems like a nice enough bloke, but his face is not the one I want to look at every morning.

After an entire day with my new PA, I need to see Rika again.

But she's exhausted. I can tell that the second she opens her door. Especially when she yawns.

"Hey," she says. "What's for dinner?"

I hold up a takeaway bag. "Chinese. I hope you like that."

"Sure." Rika yawns again. "Sounds good. Come on in."

"Maybe I should leave the food and go. You look knackered."

"Yeah, I am. But it'll be nice to have dinner with you." She moves to the side so I can walk into her flat. "I don't know how

Eddie has the energy to teach all those classes. I got wiped out just watching him."

She leads me to the sofa, where we sit down with the takeaway bag between us.

I bring out the cardboard containers that hold our food, along with plastic forks and plastic knives. "I hope you like sesame chicken. I also have Szechuan pork, kung pao chicken, dumplings, wontons, chow mein, and egg rolls."

Rika laughs while she opens the box of egg rolls. "You brought enough food for five people."

"You need nourishment after a long day at your new job."

She smiles. "You're so sweet, Dane. Thank you for bringing all this yummy food."

Her compliment makes me uncomfortable because I'm the reason she's so exhausted. I insisted she had to take another job, one that's in Connecticut. "I should've brought wine. Sorry."

"You don't have to apologize for not bringing wine." She plucks an egg roll out of the box. "Besides, if I drink wine tonight, I'll be asleep in five minutes flat."

"What's wrong with that? You need rest."

She bites off a chunk of her egg roll and chews it slowly, then she gestures at the many boxes of food. "Aren't you going to eat?"

"Yes, of course. But I think we need plates." I get up, glancing around. "Ah, where's the kitchen?"

"I'll get the plates."

"No, you will not. Point me in the right direction."

She waves toward a door on the other side of the living room. "In there. Plates are in the cabinet right next to the sink. So are the glasses."

I hurry into the kitchen and get two plates plus two glasses of water. When I return to the sofa, Rika is still working on her egg roll, biting off small chunks of it and chewing them like she's in no hurry to finish.

"Here," I say offering her a plate and a glass.

"Thank you." She sets the plate on her lap and the glass on the table. But when I try to move away, she grasps my hand. Her pale-brown eyes focus on me. "You really are so sweet. That's why I can't understand this fake dating thing. Why don't you get a real girlfriend?"

"Well, I—uh—" Fuck, I'm tongue-tied again. I use sitting down and putting food on my plate as an excuse to take a moment to get hold of myself. Not that I ever have much luck with that. Not when I'm in the same room with Rika. Or the same building. Or the same world. "Does it really matter why?"

There. I spoke five unbroken words.

Rika studies me for a moment while she finishes off her egg roll. "I can't believe you have trouble getting dates. I mean, you're gorgeous, smart, sexy, and super nice."

She thinks I'm sexy? Of course, she's not saying she wants to *have* sex with me. Or have a normal relationship with me. A woman of her caliber deserves better than a man who talked her into engaging in a fraud.

"I don't have room in my life for a real relationship," I say. "The re-launch is…complicated and time-consuming."

"You do seem stressed."

"There's a lot to do. Frankly, I have no bloody idea how to do most of it."

"But you ran your own company before signing with Bonsoir."

"That's true, but…" I focus on my plate and shift food around on it with my fork. "I had one small factory with twenty employees, and I was in charge. I hired Reese to do a single marketing campaign with online advertising. It was Chance's girlfriend who made my business a success by talking about it on her blog. Now I work for the second-largest cosmetics company in the world and have to do whatever Celeste tells me to do."

"Reese says you underestimate yourself and give everyone else the credit even when it's you who really made your company profitable."

I stare at her. Reese said that? I love my brother, but he's normally sarcastic and never says anything like that to me. The closest he ever came to giving me a compliment was when he slapped me on the shoulder and said with a smile, "Well, congrats on not cocking it up." That had been on the day I sold my ten thousandth device.

But he's told Rika I underestimate myself. I have no idea what to make of that.

"In those wedding videos," Rika says, "you were laughing and grinning. You even made a toast in which you said lots of words without a hiccup. So I know you can be well-spoken and charming. I don't buy that the only reason you don't want a real girlfriend is because you're too busy."

Should I tell her the actual reason? It's not a complete lie that I don't have time, but mostly, I got so bloody sick of women telling me I'm boring compared to my devices. The last girl who said that was not the first to criticize my bedroom skills. I couldn't stand it if Rika reached the same conclusion about me. *Why can't you be as exciting as your toys?*

"Maybe there is another reason," I say, "but we don't know each other well enough to talk about that."

"Okay, you're probably right." She consumes a bite of sesame chicken, eying me with curiosity. "It can't be a problem in bed. You're way too hot for that, a fact I can attest to since we've kissed twice."

She'll probably change her mind about that if we ever do have sex. Which is why we won't. Not ever.

We eat our dinner and talk about inconsequential things, like Rika's favorite places in New York and what Eddie Masters' house looks like. She describes his video recording studio in great detail. She's clearly excited about her new job and enjoying the challenges of working for a fitness guru.

I work out, but not as much as I'm sure Eddie Masters does. I've never seen the man, much less spoken to him, but I can tell Rika thinks he's impressive. Especially when she says those exact words right after I've thought them.

"Eddie is one impressive guy," she announces. "An entrepreneur who turned his life's passion into a successful brand." She pokes my chest with her finger. "Just like you."

"I don't have a brand yet. Celeste explained to me how a brand is different from a line of products, but I honestly can't remember half of what she said. It's all too bloody complicated." I grumble and, I suspect, make a petulant face. I don't mean to, but this re-launch and branding rubbish makes me feel like a child being led around by his mother. "Apparently, a brand involves my face on the sodding package."

"Celeste will give up on that idea, trust me."

"What makes you think that?"

"She's a good person, but sometimes she goes overboard. I've gotten to know her over the past six months, since I became good friends with her granddaughter. Eventually, Celeste will realize she needs to give you some space."

I hope she realizes that soon. Tonight would be brilliant, but I'll have to wait until Monday to find out if she's seen reason yet.

"I like Celeste," I say. "But you're right. She can be a bit too… enthusiastic."

"You mean bossy. Go on, you can say it." Rika leans toward me, her face so close to mine that I can feel her breaths tickling my skin. "Celeste Arnaud is a bossy, bossy woman. Repeat it with me. Celeste is—"

"Why would I want to repeat that? You're being ridiculous."

"Maybe. But you need some serious stress relief. Why not spend the weekend at a spa?"

"A spa? Only if you come along to help me relax."

The second those words come out of my mouth I know I've made the biggest blunder yet.

"Sorry," I rush to say. "I didn't mean—That wasn't—Ah, bollocks."

Rika smiles, like she doesn't mind my faltering speech. "Don't panic. I know you weren't suggesting we go to a spa together for a weekend of Reiki and hot sex."

I stare at her for several seconds, and my eyes start to burn because I've stopped blinking. She can't mean she wants to… No, she's making a joke. Because, obviously, the idea of her sleeping with me is ludicrous.

She pats my chest and leans back. "How about dessert?"

"I didn't think to buy dessert. Sorry."

"That's okay." Her mouth opens on a big yawn. "I've got some Oreo truffles in the freezer."

She starts to get up.

I hold up my hand to stop her. "Let me get it. I think I can manage to find the Oreo truffles on my own. I imagine they're round?"

"Yes. Round, white balls with chocolate streaks on them. They're in a plastic bag. I made them myself. The insides are full of crushed chocolate chips and white chocolate, mixed with cream cheese. Totally decadent and delicious." She licks her lips. "I love feeling those big, succulent balls in my mouth. Mm-mm-mmmmm."

"All right. I'll find them." I hurry into the kitchen because her description of how good those truffles are has roused my cock. Why on earth would she describe candy as "big, succulent balls" that she loves to feel in her mouth? Is she trying to drive me insane?

I rummage in the freezer until I find the large, plastic bag full of big, white balls. My balls will be blue in thirty seconds flat if Rika describes these truffles to me again.

After dumping the truffles onto a plate, I go back into the living room. I've just sat down on the sofa again, and I'm about to speak, when I notice her eyes are closed. She still sits sideways on the sofa, angled toward me, but her cheek rests on the back. Her breathing has become even and shallower.

Rika is asleep.

I pop a truffle into my mouth and chew it. The flavors of the semisweet chips and white chocolate merge on my tongue, and the cream cheese makes the truffle, well, creamy. It tastes delicious, like Rika said it would.

After returning the truffles to the freezer, I hunt around until I find a fleece throw, then I lay it over Rika's shoulders. She looks so beautiful sleeping, her mouth curved into the faintest smile, her face and body completely relaxed. I envy her for that. When was the last time I felt at peace? Or took a day off? I can't have a spa day or do anything else that might in the slightest resemble relaxation.

I'm too fucking busy.

Chapter Nine

Rika

I wake up after midnight and realize I'm still on the sofa, but someone has put a blanket over me. Though the floor lamp is still on, I don't see Dane anywhere. Rubbing my eyes, I yawn and sit up, looking around like I think Dane will be waiting in the armchair or something. Of course he's not. I fell asleep, so he left.

But I see a piece of folded paper that stands upright on the coffee table like a little tent. My name is written on the paper in Dane's handwriting.

Yes, I recognize his handwriting. Though I only worked for him for a few weeks, I memorized a lot of things about him. He has elegant, crisp penmanship. I envy him that because my cursive absolutely sucks.

I pick up his note and read it. Sleep well, it says, we can have those truffles another time.

A yawn overtakes me, so I carry Dane's note into my bedroom and set it on the nightstand where I can see it, then I crawl into bed. I'm gazing at the note when I fall asleep.

The next day, I decide I really ought to make sure Dane isn't holed up in his big hotel suite all alone, like the creepy loser our fake relationship is supposed to ensure nobody thinks he is. Yeah, that's the reason I wind up at the Four Seasons Hotel at ten o'clock in the morning on a Saturday. I'm making sure we keep up appearances. It has nothing to do with the fact his sweetness last night gave me a warm glow all over.

I take a private elevator all the way up to the penthouse suite. When the car stops and the doors open, Dane is standing right outside the elevator waiting for me.

"Rika, what are you doing here?" he asks. "I saw you on the camera, but you didn't ring me first to say you'd be coming."

"Um, what camera?"

"This suite has three elevators and cameras in all of them."

"Wow, that's a little spooky."

Naturally, he's wearing dress slacks and a dress shirt. At least he isn't wearing a tie, though he does have shoes on. Shiny loafers. And he has a belt too.

I remember Elena telling the story of how, the first time she visited Chance in his big hotel suite, he answered the door wearing nothing but a towel. Why couldn't Dane do that? I'm in serious need of man candy. But no, he looks like he's about to hold a meeting with foreign diplomats.

"Shouldn't you be happy to see your girlfriend?" I ask. Leaning in, I whisper, "Even if it is a sham, we should make sure everyone sees us together. Don't you think?"

"I suppose you're right."

Dane steps aside so I can walk past him.

Holy moly. I've never seen a hotel room like this one before. We're up on the fifty-second floor, with a fabulous view of the city and its skyscrapers with a blue sky as the backdrop. I wander through the huge suite, taking in the jaw-dropping views from the four glass balconies. I stop in what looks like a library. I mean, it has books on shelves, so yeah, it must be a library. The room has gorgeous golden-brown paneling, two sofas, and two chairs, not to mention a baby grand piano—and one of those glass balconies.

Dane comes up beside me, his expression neutral, like none of this opulence affects him in the least. "What should we do? To show the world we're a couple."

"Hang out, I guess. If I stay here for a while, everyone will probably assume we banged each other all day long."

"I'm not sure—That's, ah—" He scrubs a hand over his mouth. "Do we really want to give people that impression? You're not my mistress."

"Sure I am." I turn toward him and wave my hands at my body. "Arm candy here, remember? I'm just an ornament to help you prove your manliness."

"I don't like that description."

"Neither do I, but that's the deal. Right?"

"Yes, but—" He scrunches his whole face in the cutest expression of frustration and annoyance. "I don't want the world to see you that way."

"Ugh, Dane." Now I sound frustrated and probably look it too, like he had a second ago. "You can't have it both ways. I'm your fake girlfriend, but you don't want to use me as a body ornament. That's the point of this charade, isn't it? I mean, you told me this would be a business arrangement because Celeste insists you must have a woman on your arm at public events."

"You remember exactly what I said? That sounds verbatim."

"It is. I have an excellent memory."

"Yes, I can tell." He shoves his hands into his pants pockets and ambles over to the glass balcony. While he gazes out at the view, he sighs and removes his glasses. After staring at them for a minute, he puts them back on and slumps his shoulders. "This sounded like a good idea when I suggested it."

I approach him, slipping my arm under his. "Well, you can always fake dump me."

"Would you mind not making jokes about our…arrangement?" He hunches his shoulders, his gaze veering down to the floor. "I don't like to think about it."

"But you have to. We're in too deep to back out. You got me a new job and everything."

Maybe I'm secretly afraid I won't see him again if he calls off our phony relationship. I work in Connecticut now. Dane has a new PA. He won't need me anymore if we're not pretending to date. I love spending time with him, like last night when he'd brought me dinner and we sat on the sofa talking. He even put a blanket over me when I fell asleep.

He groans. "I know we can't back out of it. The wheels are already in motion. I told Celeste first thing yesterday that you and I are dating and that's why I needed a new PA." He scrunches up his face again. "I'm sure Celeste has already told Reese to start a new marketing campaign all about you and me and a lot of bollocks about how well I satisfy you in bed."

Maybe he would satisfy me—if we had sex.

Not maybe. He absolutely would fulfill my every desire. Those two make-out sessions heated me up in all the right ways. No man who kisses like that could be anything less than stellar in bed. It's not "bollocks."

"If you're so miserable," I say, "you should talk to Celeste. She cares about keeping her employees happy."

He leans against the glass balcony, his eyes aimed toward the view but his focus clearly on something much farther away. "I'll think about it."

"Okay." I'm pretty sure that when he says he'll think about it he means he's never going to do it. He seems shy about telling anyone how he's really feeling. So I decide to distract him from his worries. "Let's do something fun, like order room service. A whole bunch of totally fattening, cholesterol-laden goodies."

He eyes me sideways. "Is that meant to make me feel better? Getting nauseous from eating too much doesn't appeal to me."

"Who said you have to eat too much? Let's order everything on the breakfast menu and try all of it. No overeating unless you feel like it." I nudge him with my shoulder. "What do you say?"

"All right."

Dane makes the call to order our late breakfast. I already had breakfast when I got up this morning, but I ate light, so I've got room left for a decadent brunch. Besides, Dane needs cheering up. And I want to make him feel better. Want to so much. I would hug him, but I'm afraid that might embarrass him.

Dane says he needs to take a shower while we wait for our food. He looks clean to me, but I figure he needs some alone time. He emerges from the bathroom about a minute before the elevator doors open and a hotel employee wheels a cart full of our food through the suite and out onto the spacious balcony. The polite young man sets our food on a table. Dane gives him a tip and sends him on his way.

We don't talk much while we eat, but we do feed each other. He surprises me by starting it, holding a forkful of pancake to my lips, then slipping it inside my mouth when I open up to accept the food gift. I never would've expected Dane Dixon to do something like that. He acts so serious most of the time, but feeding me pancakes and French toast and eggs Benedict doesn't jibe with that. He knows how to relax. Huh.

When I take a sip of milk, I get clumsy and wind up dribbling some down my chin.

Dane grabs a napkin and wipes the milk off my skin, then he rubs his thumb over the corner of my mouth.

I feed him too, but he doesn't dribble anything on himself. I kind of wish he would so I can lick it off. Seeing him this way, at ease and enjoying our brunch, makes me want him even more than I already do. Okay, pretty much everything he does makes me hot for him. Yeah, I'm still massively crushing on him, and it's still pathetic.

After our meal, Dane tells me he has work to do. I point out that it's Saturday, which means it's the weekend, but he dismisses that with a shrug and a grunt. I let him have his alone time, only because he fed me breakfast, literally, using his own hand and fork.

On Sunday afternoon, I call his suite instead of just going there like I did yesterday. He informs me he doesn't have time for a visit because he has tons of work to do. Jeez, will he never take an entire day off? I don't ask him that. We're not a couple, so it's none of my business.

Why do I have to keep reminding myself of that?

Sunday evening, I'm in the middle of cleaning the toilet, elbow deep in the bowl, when the doorbell rings. I jog through my apartment and pull the door open, realizing too late that I'm still wearing big rubber gloves. At least I remembered to put down the toilet brush.

Celeste Arnaud smiles at me. "Good evening, Rika darling. We need to have a chat about Dane."

"If you've got a problem with Dane, why not talk to him?"

"Because you're the only one who can get through to him."

Me? If she knew about our make-believe relationship, she wouldn't say that. Celeste believes Dane and I are a legitimate couple and that I have some kind of sway over him.

"Come on in," I say, moving out of the way so Celeste can walk inside. "My apartment is messy right now. I'm in the middle of cleaning up."

She walks past me, turns around, and glances at my gloved hands. "Yes, I can see that. If you still worked for Bonsoir, I'd make sure you had a cleaning crew to take care of those jobs for you. Hasn't Dane offered to do that? I pay him enough that he could afford to hire you an entire team of cleaners, housekeepers, cooks, and anything else you need."

She pays him that much? I have no idea exactly how much it is, but I get the picture that it's a lot. My fake honey has no obligation to pay for anything for me. I wouldn't want him to even if we were a couple because it would make me feel weird.

Celeste and I sit down on the sofa, and I take off my big gloves.

"Dane is very stressed," she says. "I called him an hour ago, but he didn't pick up his cell, so I tried the direct line to his suite. When he answered, he sounded...rough."

"What does that mean?"

"He said he hadn't slept much last night and he's too busy with work to talk to me. I asked what work he has to do on the weekend." She smiles a little, like what she says next is almost funny. "He growled at me, then said he's working on the 'bloody devices' that I 'commanded' him to create."

"Did you command him?"

She waves a dismissive hand. "I asked him to create two new devices. That should be easy for a smart, talented man like Dane. But he's clearly more stressed than I realized." She touches my knee. "He needs your tender loving care."

"Me? I have no idea what to do to help him." But yeah, I've noticed how stressed he is too. I did my best yesterday to make him feel better. What else can I do? We're not actually dating.

Celeste doesn't know that.

Should I tell her? Oh no, not in a million years. Dane would freak if I did that.

"I told Dane I'm sorry," Celeste says, "if I put too much pressure on him. But honestly, he should've told me he was struggling. Since he's not comfortable discussing the problem with me, you are the only one who might get through to him."

Can I? No idea. Should I try? Not sure.

The clock on the wall tells me it's nine p.m., which is way too late for me to dash over to Dane's hotel and do...whatever. I need to go to bed so I can make my early morning train to Stamford. For my new job. The one Dane insisted on getting for me. He made a few passing comments yesterday that suggested he and his new PA aren't exactly hitting it off like a house on fire.

After what Celeste has told me, I'm positive the friction between Dane and his new PA isn't Noah's fault. Dane is simply too anxious to get along with anyone.

Except me. We hit it off just fine.

"Okay," I tell Celeste, "I'll talk to him. But it'll have to wait until tomorrow. I need to sleep, or I'll be useless at my new job. I will stop by Dane's hotel after work."

"Perfect." Celeste pats my knee and gets up. "I know you'll straighten him out. Every woman understands how to help her man relax."

She winks.

"Uh, sure," I say, pushing up off the sofa. "Somehow I'll relax him. Maybe a massage will help."

Celeste slants in to stare straight into my eyes from inches away. "Maybe I wasn't clear enough. Dane needs sex. Relieve his stress with an orgasm, darling, not a massage."

Then she walks out the door.

Sure, the idea of getting it on with Dane makes me tingle all over, but I can't do that. Our "relationship" is a business arrangement. I want us to give each other fantastic orgasms, over and over, like Celeste thinks I should do. I want it so much that my sex is getting slick and hot just thinking about it. I want *him*.

Maybe a good night's rest will help me figure out what to do. Give in to my lust and seduce Dane, or talk him down off that emotional ledge—then rip his clothes off and ride him until we're both sweaty and satisfied.

I give up on cleaning and relieve my own stress the Celeste Arnaud way while I fantasize about Dane Dixon.

Chapter Ten

Dane

For the entire weekend, I hide in my hotel suite and struggle to come up with ideas for the new devices I promised Celeste I'd create. I made that promise months ago, and I still have no ruddy idea what I'm going to do. I used to excel at creating sex toys that would make women feel good, but now I can't think of even one thousandth of an idea.

Why can't you be as exciting as your toys?

Those words still echo in my mind on Monday morning when I head for my office. The call I received from Celeste yesterday keeps replaying in my thoughts too, and I wonder if I am as pent up as everyone seems to think. I never used to be, but the re-launch is fraying my every nerve.

"Good morning, Mr. Dixon, sir," Noah says as I walk past his desk. He smiles too. "Can I get you some coffee?"

"Yes, please. One sugar, no cream."

While he retrieves my coffee, I shuffle into my office and drop onto my chair. My shoulders sag. I brace my elbow on the chair's arm and rest my head in my raised palm, which forces me to slump to the side. I have no energy whatsoever, not for what I need to do today. Meetings, meetings, and more meetings.

Noah brings me a cup of coffee, setting it on my desk in front of me. "Anything else I can get you?"

"No, that's all. Thank you." I sit up and glance down at my desk. "Where's the agenda for today? Rika always has it on my desk waiting for me."

"Oh, gosh, I'm sorry. I didn't know. Let me print that out for you."

He leaves, shutting the door.

And my phone rings. Will I never get a moment's peace?

I snatch up the phone. "What is it, Noah?"

Maybe I sound a touch irritable. And maybe I should apologize for that, but Noah speaks again.

"Your brother Reese is here to see you."

"Send him in, please."

I hang up the phone and wait for Reese.

He walks through the door, a casual smile on his lips and his eyes bright and clear, unlike mine which are bleary and bloodshot. Not sleeping well doesn't agree with me. My new position at Bonsoir doesn't agree with me. Noah certainly doesn't agree with me.

Rika does. Always.

"What do you want, Reese?" I ask.

He sits down in one of the chairs across the desk from me. "I hear you have a problem with the new packaging. Celeste asked me to talk to you about that."

I groan and let my head fall back against my chair. "Go on, then. Talk to me about it."

Reese sets his ankle on the opposite knee. "What's your bloody problem with the packaging?"

Though his words suggest he's annoyed, his tone of voice contradicts that. He's still smiling too. My cheerful, smiling brother waits for me to respond.

"Well, uh, I…" Now I stammer when I speak to my brother? Christ, I need a tranquilizer or…something. "I don't want my picture on the ruddy box. Or my name on it either."

Reese keeps smiling at me, though he tips his head to the side like he's trying to figure me out. "You didn't complain when Chance's girlfriend promoted you and your devices on her blog."

"That was different. She didn't show my face on the package with the words Dane's Delights printed next to it, and she didn't label me 'the man behind the O's.' She didn't order me to get a girlfriend either."

Reese chuckles. "Celeste told me about that. But you're with Rika now, aren't you? So that's one problem solved." He angles toward me and smirks. "Get Rika to shag your brains out, mate. That'll relieve all your stress."

I clench my jaw. Celeste suggested yesterday that all I need is "one good night in bed with Rika, alone and naked." Now Reese tells me the same thing, as if sex will cure all my problems.

I can't tell either of them Rika and I are only pretending to date.

So I scowl at my brother. "You always claim sex solves everything, but it's not the panacea you say it is. And I do *not* want my face or my name on the sodding package." I slam my fist down on the desk. "Do you understand, Reese?"

He raises his hands, palms out. "Take it easy, Dane. We'll remove your picture from the package, but I'll have to talk to Celeste about whether we can change the name. She won't agree to Bedroom Buddies, but if you came up with an alternative—"

"Get my name off it, Reese. Now. You're the vice president of advertising, so come up with a new name yourself."

"All right, all right. Let me work on that." Reese stands, then bends over my desk to look me in the eye. "You need a good shag, Dane. Trust me."

My brother leaves my office—while humming cheerfully.

What is wrong with me? I never yell at anyone. Certainly not my brothers. Yet here I am acting like a wounded wild beast, snarling and gnashing my teeth at anyone who gets too close.

I rest my arms on the desk and stare down at the surface. Maybe I do need a good shag, but I can't ask Rika to give me one. She doesn't really want me. She's doing me a favor by acting like my girlfriend.

What have I gotten myself into?

Groaning, rather loudly, I drop my head onto the desktop.

"Are you okay, Mr. Dixon, sir?"

Noah's voice makes me groan again.

I wave a hand in the air but keep my face on the desk. "Fine, thank you."

He doesn't leave, despite my assurance I'm fine. It's a lie, but he doesn't know that. Does he?

"Uh, I have the agenda for today, Mr. Dixon, sir." The shuffling of feet on the carpeting tells me he's moved closer. "Here it is."

I force myself to lift my head, and I see the paper he's set on my desk, just above where my head had been lying. "Thank you, Noah."

He turns to leave.

Groaning yet again, I mutter, "I need to get pissed."

Noah stops halfway to the door, turning toward me. "You're really mad, huh?"

"What? No, not really. I said I want to get pissed."

His eyes flare wide for a split second. "Oh, I get it. Sorry, I don't do that."

"You don't do what?"

He gestures toward his groin with both hands, flapping one hand with his fingers curled like he's cupping his dick. "You know, the golden shower thing. I don't do that."

For a moment, all I can do is stare at him. Then the meaning of his statement hits me like a snowball lobbed at my face.

I growl, and that's not a metaphor or an exaggeration. I literally growl at him. "I don't want you to piss *on* me. I want to *get* pissed. Which means I have a strong urge to get drunk."

Not that I think it will help. Can't hurt, can it?

"Oh, sorry," Noah says. "I don't do that either."

I brace my elbows on the desktop and cradle my face in my raised hands. "That will be all, Noah."

His footsteps assure me he's left my office.

After several minutes of sitting here with my head in my hands, I realize what I need. Not sex. I just need to see Rika. Why, I have no bloody idea. But I need it so badly that once I think of the idea, I find myself getting up out of my chair and stalking out to Noah's desk.

"I have a dentist appointment," I say, lying much more convincingly than I'd thought I could. "I'll be back this afternoon."

Noah glances down at his desk calendar, and the corner of his mouth crimps. "I don't see it on the agenda."

"That's because I made the appointment myself on Friday, after Rika left. I forgot to tell you."

"Okay, sure. Have a good dentist appointment."

Does anyone have a good time at the dentist?

I hurry out of the building and drive all the way to Stamford, breaking the speed laws the whole time. I don't get pulled over by a policeman, thankfully. By the time I park in Eddie Masters' driveway, I'm beginning to feel odd about this. What will Rika say when I turn up at her workplace? She'll probably think I've lost my mind.

Which I have.

The door opens seconds after I ring the bell.

A middle-aged woman dressed in a maid's uniform smiles at me. "How may I help you?"

"I'm here to see"—I swallow hard—"my girlfriend, Rika Solberg. She works for Mr. Masters."

"Oh sure, hon, come on in."

The woman leads me through the house to a set of sliding glass doors that access a large patio. I thank her, and she leaves.

Out on the patio, Rika stands in her bare feet with one foot on the ground and the other leg raised behind her, with her arms outstretched. One arm is horizontal to the ground while the other is perpendicular to it. She wears only leggings and a tank top, with her hair tied up in a ponytail.

And Eddie Masters has his hands on her.

My fists clench all on their own. I can't think clearly enough to fist my hands on purpose, because that man has one hand on Rika's thigh and the other on her hip. He says something that makes her laugh, then he pats her hip.

I storm out onto the patio and stop just past the glass doors. "What the bloody hell is going on here?"

Rika's gaze swerves to me, and all the happiness floods out of her expression. "Dane? What are you doing here?"

"The better question is what is that tosser doing with his hands all over you? You're my girlfriend."

Eddie Masters backs away from Rika, holding his hands up. "Hey, relax. Nothing's going on here."

Rika stomps up to me looking like she wants to throttle me with both hands. She seizes my arm and tows me into the house. As we cross the threshold into the living room, she tells Eddie, "Sorry about this. Gimme a minute, okay?"

"Sure, no problem."

We make it halfway across the living room before she forces me to halt and slams her palms onto my chest. "What is your problem? Showing up at my work to snarl at my boss? What the hell, Dane?"

I've never seen Rika angry. She's always polite and happy.

But I'm behaving like a sodding arsehole. Of course she's angry. I deserve whatever she wants to do to me.

"He had his hands on you," I say. "That looked like sexual harassment to me. Since you had an employer treat you that way once before, I don't want to see it happen again."

Maybe that is a small part of it, but mostly, I hated seeing another man touching her when I can't do that.

The anger seems to flood out of her, and her shoulders slump. She sighs and rolls her head in a circle, like she's working out kinks in her neck. "Okay, fine, I can see how you might think that. But I don't believe concern for me was the main reason you shouted at Eddie."

Maybe I should be honest, but I can't make the words come out of my mouth. "I—well—it, uh—"

She holds up a hand. "Please stop. I forgive you, it's over, we're cool."

I glance at the patio, where Eddie seems to be doing tai chi. "I'm sorry. It's just that every man who sees you wants you. You're beautiful, sexy, and clever. I wouldn't blame Eddie Masters if he did make a pass."

She snorts, clearly trying to contain her laugher. "You don't need to worry about Eddie."

"He's a man, and you're a beautiful woman."

Rika smiles and lays her hand on my chest. "You're so cute, but you really have nothing to worry about. Eddie's gay."

"Are you having me on?"

"No, he's really gay. And he's way too nice to sexually harass anyone." She leans in closer. "For the record, Eddie had his hands on me because he was giving me a yoga lesson."

"Oh. Maybe I should, ah, apologize to him."

"Let me handle that. Don't you need to be at work?"

"Yes, I do."

She waves her hand. "Then go."

I go, and I violate the speed laws again on my way back to work.

Noah almost cringes when I step out of the elevator, heading toward his desk and my office. I pass him without glancing at or speaking to him. What can I say? *Sorry I made you think I wanted you to urinate on me, then I snarled at you.* I'd scared Noah. The bloke has known me for less than two days, and I've made a brilliant first impression.

Well, I can kiss that Boss of the Year trophy goodbye.

After fifteen minutes of glaring down at my desk and cursing at myself in my thoughts, I realize what I need to do. *One* thing I need to do, that is. Most everything else… I've got no fucking idea.

I approach Noah's desk.

He stops blinking and darts his gaze everywhere but at me. "What can I do for you, Mr. Dixon, sir?"

"Noah, I…" Scrubbing a hand over my mouth, I try to figure out what to say. "I'm sorry for the way I behaved earlier. You didn't do anything wrong. It's entirely my fault."

"Oh. Thank you, Mr. Dixon, sir."

"Call me Dane, please."

His eyes are large, but he sounds happier when he says, "Sure. Thank you, Dane."

The elevator doors open, and Rika steps out.

Before I can summon the brainpower to comprehend the fact she's here, she takes hold of my tie and leads me into my office using my tie as a leash.

When we cross the threshold, she says, "Close the door."

I kick it shut while I follow her around my desk to my chair. What is she doing? Her bossy tone when she ordered me to close the door made my cock wake up. What she's wearing wakes it up even more. She still has on the leggings and tank top, but now she's added running shoes and a long, open sweater that hangs down to her knees. Her ponytail bounces with every step she takes.

And I imagine grasping that ponytail while I fuck her.

She stops beside my chair and releases my tie. "Sit down."

"Why are you here? Don't you need to be at work?"

"I told Eddie I need the rest of the day off to take care of my boyfriend. He lent me his Corvette so I could get here faster." She wags a finger at me. "No more talking. I'm here to relieve your stress, Dane. So sit down and shut up."

Relieve my stress? If she means to talk me into meditating or doing yoga…

She grabs my tie again and hauls me closer, with only a hair's breadth between our bodies. "You'll want to be sitting down when I do this. Otherwise, your knees might buckle. For sure, your eyes will roll back in your head."

I sit down.

Rika kneels in front of me, crawling forward on her knees until she's wedged between my thighs. She undoes my tie and tosses it onto the desk, then she unhooks the top button on my shirt.

Suddenly, I'm having trouble breathing. My cock is hard. She can't mean to have sex with me here in my office. Why would she make me sit down for that, anyway? I want to fuck her on my desk, up against the window, on the floor, any way she'll let me have her.

Rika unfastens my belt, frees the button on my trousers, and slides the zipper down so slowly that watching her do it makes me breathe harder, faster, my mouth open and my whole body tense with anticipation. She bends toward me, her lips grazing my ear as she whispers, "I'm really good at doing this."

"Doing…what?"

She pulls back so I can see her face, and her lips curl into the sexiest little smile I've ever seen. "Prepare to have your mind blown." She glances down at my groin. "And other parts of you too."

No, she can't mean to—

Rika pulls my dick out of my trousers and shorts, cupping it in her soft, warm hand. "Oh wow, you're so big and hard and hot. Can't wait to swallow you whole."

Fuck. She means to do what I thought she meant to do. The thought of her mouth on me… I may not last long once she starts.

She strokes me with one hand, humming like she can't wait to consume me, and with her other hand she massages my inner thigh.

"Rika, I—"

Her tongue rakes across the head of my erection.

I jerk and gasp, gripping my chair's arms so tightly my fingers ache, but I don't care. Her tongue, it's velvety and warm and moist. When she flicks it out to tease me again, I let out a choked sound. My ears are ringing, and she hasn't even gotten to what I know will be the best part.

"Mm," she moans, licking her lips.

"You'd better hurry. I can't—I won't—make it much longer."

Rika closes her fist around the base of my cock. "Time to blow your mind."

She opens her mouth and does exactly what she said. She swallows me whole, taking me deep inside. Her soft moans vibrate my flesh while she sucks gently and moves her mouth up and down, up and down, flicking her tongue as she moves. Her hand pumps me too, her smooth palm so fucking arousing I've lost all capacity to speak, to think, or to breathe.

My back bows. The pressure builds and builds while she starts to suck me more forcefully, her moans turning into grunts while her eyes drift half closed like she loves doing this to me.

She won't swallow when I come. Women never want to do that, at least not with me.

"Fuck, Rika."

The orgasm rips through me, hot and hard and so bloody incredible that I squeeze my eyes shut and let out a long, rasping shout. When it's over, I'm breathing hard and so limp that all I can do is lie here slouched in my chair.

But I've never felt better in my entire life.

I gaze at Rika, probably looking dazed, because I am.

She slides her tongue over her lips like she's lapping up every last bit of what I spent in her mouth. "Mm, you're the best thing I've ever tasted. And I love the way you look when you come."

"Rika, that was…amazing."

"Do you feel more relaxed now?"

"I can honestly say I've never been more relaxed in my life." I cup her cheek in one hand. "You are the most wonderful woman in the world."

She laughs, the sound delicate and sweet. "You're adorable when you're satisfied."

As I gaze into her golden eyes, with those green flecks sparking in the sunlight that streams through the windows, I realize exactly what I need to do.

I bend forward to wrap my arms around her waist and lift her up with me. Once we're both standing, I pull her snug against me.

"It's your turn, Rika."

Chapter Eleven

Rika

Dane backs me up to the desk, slips his hands under my ass, and lifts me onto the desk so I'm perched on its edge. It's my turn, he said. Oh God, I hope he means what I think he means. I got so turned on when I had him in my mouth, and the look on his face only made me hotter for him. What I want most of all is for Dane to thrust into me and make us both come.

His slacks are still undone, and his dick hangs between our bodies.

I need that inside me. But I also want his mouth on me, and I can't decide which I want first.

Dane kneels between my thighs. He pulls my leggings down, and I lift my hips to help him, until they're lumped around my ankles, trapped by my shoes. He glides his hands up my calves, his skin grazing mine and setting off a wave of tingling heat in its wake. He places a soft kiss on each knee, then sweeps his hands over them and up my thighs.

He hooks his fingers inside the waist of my panties and drags them down too.

I spread my legs more for him. Oh God, I'm so wet and ready that it's almost embarrassing. I wanted him the day we met, but I've been desperately crushing on him since that day in the restaurant. It's become more than a crush, though. I might be kind of obsessed with his body.

Dane takes his glasses off, sets them on the desk, and lowers his head between my legs. The first touch of his tongue makes me gasp and grip the desk's edge. When he drags his tongue up and down my cleft, my breaths turn into sharp gasps, one after another after another.

"Oh yes, Dane." I clasp his head with both hands while he swirls his tongue around my clitoris without touching it. "Please, yes, please."

He laps at the slick skin just below my clit, his nose brushing that hard nub. When he finally closes his mouth around it, an electric current fires through my body, exciting every nerve. Holy shit, Dane knows what he's doing. I've had guys do this before, but none of the others got me so excited so fast. When he thrusts a finger inside me, I start panting and dig my nails into his scalp. He licks faster, sucks harder, thrusts that finger deeper, until I'm teetering on the edge. So close, almost there.

"Yes, Dane, more," I plead between panting breaths.

Dane pushes two fingers inside me now, while he keeps lapping and suckling me, and I bite back a cry when he groans against my clitoris, vibrating that most sensitive part of me. A coil inside my body winds tighter and tighter, and I get wetter and wetter, so desperate for release that I'm clamping my lips shut to muffle my frantic noises. A fevered flush sweeps over me from head to toe, and I go rigid, frozen in that blissfully torturous moment before I tumble over the edge.

"Dane!" I cry out, oblivious to the fact there's a stranger right outside the door to this office. I don't give a damn who hears me. The pleasure rolling through me consumes my focus, making me shut my eyes while my body bows inward, my knees draw up, and I let out a hoarse, wordless cry.

The orgasm fades gradually, but Dane and I stay frozen with my body curled around him and his head between my legs. After a minute or two, he kisses his way down my thighs and sits back on his heels.

He drags his tongue across his lips three times like he's savoring the taste of me.

"Wow, Dane," I say, still kind of breathless from what he did to me. "That was… I can't even think of a word that's good enough to describe it. I've never come that hard before."

"You gave me the same gift. This was reciprocity."

He's got to be joking, right? Reciprocity? It was so much more than that.

Dane rises, zips up his pants, and snags his tie from the desktop. While he works on doing up his tie, he says, "I feel much better now. Thank you."

I'm sitting here on his desk, my pants and underwear around my ankles, and he thanks me. What the fuck?

"Let's go to lunch," I say, because I have no clue how I'm supposed to respond to his gratitude for the blow job I gave him.

"I don't have time." Done with his tie, he buttons his pants and secures his belt. "I'm sure Eddie wants his Corvette back."

"He said I can bring it back to him tomorrow." I hop off the desk and pull up my leggings and panties. "I told Eddie I need the rest of the day off. That means we are spending time together. You go tell Noah you'll be out of the office until tomorrow."

Dane looks at me with a bland expression. "I don't have time for—"

I seal two fingers over his mouth to shut him up. "I get that we just had a very intimate encounter and you're feeling off kilter because of that. But I am not letting you get away with dismissing it as nothing."

"Have I called it nothing?"

"No, but you're acting like that."

"You said you were going to relax me, you did it, and I can't see what else there is to say. It was a casual thing."

Casual? Is he out of his ever-loving mind? The way he brought me to climax had been the single most intense sexual experience of my life.

His face has gone stoic, though, and he pats my arm like I'm a puppy he just gave a tummy rub. "This was nice. Thank you."

Then he waltzes toward the door.

"Hey!" I shout.

Dane freezes with his hand on the doorknob, turning only his eyes to look at me. His wide, stunned eyes.

I stomp up to him, stabbing my finger into his chest. "You do not get to walk away like getting a blow job in your office is an everyday thing."

He flinches the tiniest bit.

"We shared an intense experience," I say. "It wasn't casual. I get that you're terrified of that, though I have no idea why, but being your fake girlfriend does not make me your on-call plaything."

"You're not—I never said—That's—" He screws up his entire face, drops his head onto the door with a thump, and groans.

Oh jeez, now he looks so pitiful that I want to hug him. This man has more tension and angst inside him than I ever realized until this moment. And I feel for him. More than I should, probably. But I can't help it.

"You need a break," I say. "Celeste came to see me last night, and she's worried you're putting too much pressure on yourself. I'm worried about you too. Let's go back to your hotel, cuddle up on one of those big sofas, and order a bunch of decadent desserts from room service."

"I can't," he moans with his head still resting on the door. "There's too much to do."

"Come on, Dane. You need more than oral sex, and I want to help you, so let me." I bite my lip, studying him and his defeated posture. "Okay, I'm just going to do it."

He lifts his head, his brows cinched up tight. "Do what?"

"This." I throw my arms around him, resting my chin on his shoulder. "I've never met anyone who needs a hug more than you do."

"I..." He trails off like he has no idea what to say.

So I keep myself mashed to his body, my arms around his neck, and breathe in the scent of him. He's not wearing cologne, but he smells good naturally. He feels good too. I can't remember the last time I hugged anyone, and I think I'm getting as much comfort from it as I hope he will.

Little by little, his body softens. His head lowers, and his cheek brushes against mine. A breath gusts out of him as he links his hands at the small of my back.

We stand there like that for a minute or two, maybe longer. I lose track of the time because this is the nicest thing I've done in ages. Why do I love cuddling with Dane? I'm not sure, but I'm also not sure it matters. This feels so good and so right that I don't want to examine the reasons why.

"All right," he says on another, gustier sigh that flutters my hair. "Let's go to my suite and…do whatever."

I suppose "or whatever" is the closest he'll ever come to admitting he wants to snuggle with me on a big sofa. I'll take it.

Without letting go of me, Dane opens the door and announces, "Noah, I'm taking the rest of the afternoon off. You should too. I'll make sure you're paid for the full day."

"Thank you, Mr. Dixon, sir," Noah says. "Sorry. I meant Dane."

"Enjoy your afternoon."

Dane keeps an arm around my waist as he leads me to the elevator. The car is empty, and once the doors glide shut, Dane pulls me snug against his gorgeous body and kisses me. The second our mouths collide I hum with pleasure and excitement. I love kissing him, though we've only done this a few times before. I love the sensation of his mouth on mine, of his tongue diving between my lips to tease me and arouse me, and of his hands splayed over my upper back. He takes it slow like he's in no hurry, like we can do this all afternoon.

And I guess we can. He's taken the rest of the day off.

When we exit the elevator into the lobby, I feel so deliciously warm and relaxed and turned on at the same time. This desire is softer than a little while ago in his office. I want him, but mostly, I want to spend time with him. Get to know him. Find out what he wants and needs and feels deep inside.

Which sounds an awful lot like legitimate dating.

And yeah, that's exactly what I want.

But does he want that?

Chapter Twelve

Dane

What am I doing? Taking an afternoon off during the most critical time in my career? The re-launch of my brand of sexual wellness devices is coming up sooner than I'd like, sooner than I can handle. Celeste has hammered it into me that these next weeks will make or break the re-launch, but then she tells Rika I'm stressed out and she's worried about me.

I can't blame Celeste for all my stress. I've done this to myself, haven't I? She warned me what it would be like if I signed a contract with Bonsoir. She never glossed over the downsides or what I would be expected to do. But now… I have no bloody idea how to deal with all of this.

Maybe that explains why I talked a clever, sweet, beautiful, sexy woman into pretending to date me.

When we get to my suite, Rika takes my hand and guides me into the library where we do exactly what she suggested. We snuggle on the sofa. I take off my jacket, tie, and loafers while she kicks off her shoes. She tucks her legs under her and leans against me, so I put my feet on the table and drape my arm over her shoulders. She's warm and smells like powder or…something. It's a pleasant scent. She always smells good, a fact that makes me want to shag her all the time.

I haven't done that yet. Why not?

Because it would be wrong, that's way. I want to smack my forehead with my palm, but I don't. Rika will think I've gone completely insane if I do that. But I am an idiot, to say the least, for thinking for even one second that I deserve to sleep with this woman. She should have a real boyfriend, not an arse like me who tells her it's only for show.

"What are you so afraid of?" she asks, not sounding at all irritated, despite the fact I hurt her feelings earlier.

I open my mouth to tell her I have no idea what she's talking about, but I stop short of saying it. Am I afraid? If I am, why is that?

Why can't you be as exciting as your toys?

My head falls back against the sofa like it's transformed into a granite ball and I can't hold it upright anymore. I should tell her the truth, shouldn't I? But I can't make the words come out, so instead I say, "I'd rather not talk about myself."

"That seriously limits the conversation." She wriggles until she's turned partway toward me, though she stays under my arm and nestles against me. "Tell me about your family, then. Please."

"You know my brothers."

"Not well."

I shrug my shoulder, the one she's not tucked up against. "Reese is incessantly cheerful and irritating. Chance is mature and irritating."

"Oh come on, I know you get along with your brothers. Why are you calling them irritating?"

"Because they both insist on telling me I've lost my sense of humor and I've become…" I grimace. "Uptight."

"That's because you are uptight. I'm not criticizing, but remember, I've seen the wedding videos. You were smiling and laughing, dancing with all the ladies. You even told jokes during your best man speech for Chance. Funny jokes." She nudges me with her elbow. "I know the way you are now isn't how you usually act."

"Maybe it isn't, but I can't change the way I am."

"Because you're completely stressed out."

I drum my fingers on my thigh. "Fine, yes, I'm stressed out and uptight and not any fun at all anymore."

"Admitting you have a problem is the first step to recovery."

"This isn't an AA meeting."

"No, it's a private session with your personal counselor." She points at herself. "That would be me."

"We're not actually dating, which means you aren't required to counsel me."

"I want to help you, Dane. If you'll let me."

"And what is it you think you can do for me?" I grunt and shake my head. "Even my parents think I'm on the verge of a nervous breakdown. They told me so in an email because I've been avoiding their calls."

"You need to talk to your family, not avoid them. You work in the same building as your brother Reese. Talk to him."

I clear my throat while I avoid looking at her. "I can't. I sort of, ah, shouted at Reese earlier today. Told him I don't want my face on the sodding package for my devices. And I might also have slammed my fist down on the desk when I said it."

"Reese isn't mad at you, I'm sure. He looks up to you."

"Are you sure you're talking about the same Reese? Maybe you've got my brother confused with someone else."

She laughs, and it sounds almost affectionate. "I've met your brother, in person, with his wife. Arden wouldn't hang on anyone else's body. And Reese told me, face to face, that he admires and respects you and wishes he could be more like you."

"He wants to be an uptight arsehole? I rather doubt that."

"The way you were before Bonsoir gobbled up your company."

Celeste's company gobbled up mine because I served it to Bonsoir with garnish and red wine sauce. What had I been thinking? I want to rewind the months to that moment and say no this time when Celeste offers to make me an instant billionaire.

But I can't. I'm trapped.

Rika places a hand on my cheek and touches her lips to mine.

The kiss is soft and sweet, but the feel of her skin on mine makes me want to deepen the kiss, to taste every millimeter of her mouth and explore all the ways I can excite her. I want to hear her moan and feel the vibrations of it through our fused mouths.

I can't move, though. I can't do anything except relax my lips and let her kiss me.

She pushes her tongue inside, flicking it until her teasing compels me to dive deep into her mouth and do what I thought of doing seconds ago. I devour her. And when she moans into my mouth the way I wanted her to, I feel the vibrations just how I'd imagined I might. The sensation is even better than I expected, even more arousing. I thrust a hand into her hair and pull her even closer so I can plunge deeper into the hot, silky depths of her mouth. Christ, that sounds idiotic. Hot, silky depths? But that's what she feels like. I've never loved kissing any other woman as much as I love kissing this woman.

Rika pulls away, but only enough to look me in the eye. She slides her tongue across her bottom lip. "Let's have sex, Dane."

"What? I, uh… What?" She can't mean it. I must have misheard her, or she must have misspoken.

"I said let's have sex." She swings her leg over me so she's straddling my lap, then she wraps her arms around my neck, her mouth so close I could take her bottom lip between my teeth and suck on it. "You want me. I want you. We've proved we have chemistry. We're adults, and there's no reason in the world why we shouldn't go all the way."

"But—"

She seals my lips with one finger. "You'll feel lots better when you stop fighting this attraction. Do I have to be blunt about it? Well okay, I will." She moves even closer, her breasts crushed against my chest and her lips skimming mine when she speaks. "Fuck me, Dane."

Chapter Thirteen

Rika

I can't believe I said that. *Fuck me, Dane.* I've never spoken those words to any man, but I calmly told Dane Dixon that's what I want. Okay, yeah, it is what I want. I've craved this man since the day we met, but I'm not the kind of girl who asks a man to have sex with her in such bold, explicit terms. I really hope I haven't scared him because I want to sleep with him.

And I don't care that it's afternoon and we won't fall asleep once we're done. I want Dane. Right here, right now, no more waiting. So what if our relationship is a sham? We can still have earth-shattering sex.

What happens when an uptight man lets go? I've never been with anyone like Dane before, so I have no idea. But my gut tells me sex with him will be fantastic.

"All right," he says with a sigh. "I'll do it."

He sounds…resigned.

Oh yeah, that's super sexy. *Not.*

"What's wrong?" I ask.

"I need to get—" He sighs again, shakes his head, and frowns. "One moment. Stay here."

He pushes me off his lap and gets up, walking out of the library.

Ohhhh-kay. What just happened? He agrees to having sex but says it like he's preparing for a root canal, then he leaves the room.

Dane comes back a minute later holding a plastic grocery bag full of things I can't make out.

"Everything okay?" I ask.

He shrugs one shoulder and drops onto the sofa. Offering me the bag, he says, "This is what you want."

I gingerly accept the bag, taking it by the plastic straps, and peer inside. It contains a selection of vibrators. "What is this?"

"It's what you want."

"You said that a second ago, but I still have no idea why you're giving me vibrators."

"Because you want me to fuck you."

For several seconds, I stare at him with my mouth open. Vibrators? I asked him to have sex with me. Why does he think I want toys? Something else is going on here, but I know I won't convince him to tell me what that is until after we get it on.

I set the bag of toys on the table and crawl onto his lap again. "We can play with those later if you want, but I need *you* inside me, Dane, not your toys."

He watches me, his eyes shifting this way and that like he's trying to determine if I'm telling the truth. "You mean that?"

"Yes, I do." I let my entire body sag against him, my lips ghosting over his. "I don't care where we do it as long as we do it *right now.*"

He clasps the back of my head and kisses me. It's rough and hot and so damn good that I moan and rock my hips into him, desperate to have him inside me.

Dane flips me onto my back, spread lengthwise across the sofa with my feet on his lap. He doesn't even bother unbuttoning his shirt. He tears it off over his head and flings it away. Then he gets rid of his pants and underwear, his socks too. On his knees, naked and aroused, he rakes his hooded gaze over me from head to toe.

His steamy appraisal makes me so wet and achy for him that a tingle sweeps over my entire body. I'm about to get what I've wanted since day one. I bite down on my lip while I admire the view of him. Dane has muscles—oh yes, lots and lots of delicious muscles that I want to explore with my tongue—but the part of him that robs me of breath hangs between his hips. That beautiful, thick, long cock is hard and ready for action, its tip rosy and glistening.

Oh yes, please, give me that.

I've had his dick in my mouth, but I didn't get a good look at it earlier today. I'd been too obsessed with making him come to take the time to admire that gorgeous cock.

Dane removes my socks and hooks his fingers inside the waistband of my leggings and my panties. He tugs both down to my ankles. "Think I'll leave you like this for now."

The fact that he wants my ankles bound by my leggings, like he had earlier in his office, makes me even wetter. I have no idea what he plans to do to me, and I don't care.

He crouches over me on his hands and knees. "Take off your shirt and bra."

I get rid of them faster than I've ever stripped before. Yeah, I want him like crazy, remember? I've wanted him for what feels like forever, though it's only been a few weeks. Lying naked under him with that beautiful hard-on dangling between our bodies, I'm so damn ready for this.

"Bend your knees," he commands.

And I do it. Bending my knees forces me to spread my thighs. With my ankles caught in my own clothes, I can't wrap my legs around his hips the way I want to, but it doesn't matter. Any second, he'll take me. He'll fuck me. He'll do whatever the hell he wants to do to me, and I'll love it.

He freezes, not even blinking. "Bollocks."

"What's wrong?"

"Condom. I didn't—we need—I, ah, don't, um, have—"

"My pants pocket."

His brows squish together. "What?"

"Check my pants pocket." I've kept a condom on hand ever since I met Dane. Eternally hopeful, that's me.

He fumbles with my leggings, since they're lumped around my ankles, and finally extracts the item we both want.

A condom packet.

Dane looks so adorably relieved and gets the condom on in a matter of seconds.

Then he's over me again, his hands at either side of my head, his gaze locked on mine. He thrusts into me, consuming my body with one long, slow, sensuous stroke that makes me gasp and arch my back. Oh God, this feels even better than I'd imagined all those times when I fantasized about Dane fucking me while I got off with a vibrator. He's so firm and hot, and when he's buried himself as deep as he can go, he pauses there so we can both revel in the sensations of our bodies joined at last.

He kisses me tenderly, then he dips his head to latch on to my nipple, loving it with his lips and his tongue until I'm squirming and clutching his head. The heat of his intimate kiss robs me of breath. I grasp his biceps, gazing into his blue eyes and letting them lure me down into a warm pool of liquid desire.

Releasing my nipple, he begins to move, pulling his hips back and lunging them forward in a powerful rhythm, and I abandon myself to the moment. Since I can't grip him with my legs, I grip his arms even harder and let him do whatever he wants. My sex gets even slicker and molds to his length, creating a wet sucking sound with every thrust. He hisses in a breath every time he pulls out, until only the head of his cock brushes my entrance, then the air gusts out of his lungs when he plunges inside me again, over and over and over.

"Oh yes, Dane, yes," I gasp. "You feel so good, so incredible, don't ever stop."

He lowers onto his elbows, dropping his head to my shoulder.

And he keeps going. Every lush stroke ramps up my need, and I sling my arms around him, determined to hang on to him until the very end. But I never want this to end. I need him filling me up forever, so I'll never stop experiencing the sensations he evokes in me with every little movement. When he shoves a hand under my ass and lifts it, his strokes become slower, more sensual, though he's driving even deeper into my body.

"Rika," he groans into my ear. "I need you, Rika."

"I'm here." I turn my head just enough that my lips touch his ear. "I'm not going anywhere. Please, Dane, please don't ever stop."

He groans, and the sound is so husky, so intense, that my clit throbs. "Have to—ah. Can't wait—"

"Then don't wait. Do it now, please, make us both come."

Dane slips his fingers between our bodies to separate my folds, and suddenly, I feel him even more with every stroke. He rubs that aching bud, the one that makes me writhe and cry out, and he keeps rubbing until every muscle in my body tenses in anticipation of the release I feel coming, like a train barreling straight toward a cliff, faster and faster every second, about to plummet over the edge.

At the instant I go off, he hoists himself up on his straight arms and punches into me so hard and so deep that I come even more fiercely, my body clenching his length in rolling waves of pleasure. While my nails sink into his flesh, I scream his name and squeeze my eyes shut, overwhelmed by the power of my climax, and I feel him come apart inside me.

"Rika!"

His hoarse shout echoes in the library.

I peel my lids open, still gasping for breath.

Dane is crouching over me, though his arms are shaking like he's too exhausted to hold himself up anymore but doesn't want to crush me with his body.

"Lay yourself on top of me," I say. "I want to feel you all over me. Please."

His brows do that squishing-up thing again, but after a couple seconds, he lowers his body onto mine.

The weight and heat of him feels heavenly.

With his head on my chest, he caresses my arm with his fingertips.

I comb my fingers through his hair. "That was so unbelievably spectacular. You are one incredible lover, Dane Dixon."

He tenses up, like I've told him something bad instead of paying him an awesome compliment.

"What's wrong?" I ask. "Most guys would love to be told they're fantastic lovers."

"It's, ah…" He lifts his head, searching my gaze. "You mean that, don't you?"

"That you were incredible? Hell yes, I mean it." I run my fingers over his lips. "Why does that surprise you?"

"I've, uh, been taken—been told—" He buries his face between my breasts and groans miserably. When he looks at me again, he's got the cutest befuddled expression on his face. "You really liked being with me?"

"No, Dane, I *loved* it."

He pushes up off me and sits back on his heels near my feet. "You're the only woman who has ever told me I'm spectacular and incredible. The others had…less-kind words for how sex with me made them feel."

I sit up and get rid of my leggings and panties, then I scoot closer to him. "What do these other women tell you?"

"Why can't you be as exciting as your toys. That's what they say."

Chapter Fourteen

Dane

I slump into the corner of the sofa, my legs hanging off the edge, while I watch Rika and wait for her to say she agrees with the idea that I'm not as exciting as a vibrator. She already said she loved being with me. The way she came, it was the most beautiful thing I've ever seen, and her expression evinced wonder and joy and total satisfaction. She loved it. So why am I still convinced she'll change her mind?

Rika climbs onto my lap again, her hands resting on my thighs. "About these incredibly stupid women you've been with…"

"They weren't stupid. I failed to live up to their expectations, and that's my fault."

"Bullshit." She shakes her head. "After what we just did, how can you still believe you suck at sex? Those brain-dead twerps are obnoxious, rude, and completely wrong for you."

Nothing with Rika feels wrong, despite the fact I keep insisting we're not really dating. Our fake relationship feels more real than anything I've had with other women, even the ones who didn't tell me I'm not as exciting as a sex toy.

"Maybe you're right," I say, "but I can't get over being uptight because we had one fantastic shag."

"No, it'll take lots and lots of shags." She clasps my hands to her breasts. "You need to do me several more times. And we should order a big dinner with dessert, because we are going to be burning some serious calories."

This woman wants me—again and again and again.

And fuck, I want her too. All day, all night, for the rest of the week, the month, the year.

Can we have sex nonstop for an entire year? If we take the occasional break to eat…who knows?

Rika grins.

"What's so funny?" I ask.

"It's not funny. It's a miracle." She cradles my face in her palms. "You're smiling, Dane."

"Am I?" I touch the corners of my mouth like I'm checking for a smile. "Look at that. I am smiling. Let's order champagne to toast the occasion."

Her grin gets even wider and brighter. "I knew you had a sense of humor underneath that uptight shell."

"You knew because my brothers told you."

"No, I knew because I saw through that shell."

Her words send a chill through me. She saw through me? For a moment, the idea makes me uneasy—until I realize it's not a bad thing. Rika is getting to know me. Maybe she understood me, at least a little bit, from the start. No other woman bothered to do that.

The chill gives way to a gentle warmth as I look into her eyes and tell her something I thought I'd never admit to anyone. "I don't have a problem getting dates, but everything after that point has always been…troublesome."

"In what way?"

"Women are usually disappointed in me, either because being a mechanical engineer is too boring for them or because I'm not as exciting as the devices I design."

She slides off my lap to sit beside me, her head on my chest.

I hold her close and tell her the rest. "Women don't want to hear about mechanical engineering. But what else can I talk about? It's my job, my life. If I don't say anything about that, all I have left to talk about is my family. Women don't like to hear me banging on about that either. Over the last couple of years, since my company became somewhat successful, women only want to talk about my devices."

"And then these moronic women decide they like your toys but not you."

"Yes. The problem will only get worse once the company relaunches as a branch of Bonsoir."

"Why do you think it will get worse?"

I sit forward, my elbows on my knees, while I remember the past six months. "It's already gotten worse. Every woman I've tried to date since I signed the Bonsoir contract only wants my sex toys, not me. I can't have a real relationship."

"Of course you can."

"You don't understand—"

"I get that you're convinced it's true, but that's a big old armful of hooey." She scoots forward to sit beside me, laying her head on my shoulder. "You already have a real relationship."

"Have you not been paying attention? The only woman I've been with is you, and that's all for show."

"Yeah, I know." She straightens and clears her throat. "Our relationship is not fake. Maybe we both convinced ourselves it was, but it's not. I am your girlfriend, Dane. For real."

I glance at her, unable to form any words in response. My girlfriend? Rika? I've kept telling her it's fake, that I don't have time for more, that this is strictly for publicity. Except I haven't taken her out in public more than twice. I've treated her like an employee, not a lover. Haven't I?

We had a romantic dinner at a posh restaurant. We gave each other mind-blowing climaxes in my office. I've kissed her, even when no one else was there to see it. I got jealous when a waiter spoke to her in French and when Eddie Masters put his hands on her. We hardly know each other, but maybe…

Maybe I do want more with her. More than a farce. Maybe I want her, full stop—as my lover and my girlfriend.

"I want to have a genuine relationship with you, Rika," I hear myself saying. "But I couldn't stand it if one day you tell me I'm not as exciting as my sex toys."

She slides off the sofa to kneel on the floor between my legs. "I would never say that. First of all, I haven't used any of your toys. Second, there is no way on earth any mechanical device could do better than you. The way you made me come, on this sofa and in your office, those were the best sexual experiences I've ever had." She taps her finger on my chest. "And you did that, not your devices."

"Yes, but—"

"No, Dane. You do not get to downplay what we've done together. It's real." She takes my face in her hands again. "I want you, not your devices. To prove I mean that, I'm ordering you to fuck me repeatedly until you believe it."

I laugh, and I can't remember the last time I did that. "You're ordering me to fuck you? Again? I can honestly say that has never happened to me once before today, much less twice." I smirk when I add, "Well, Reese did tell me the cure for my problems is to have you shag my brains out."

"Reese is a smart man." She unfurls her voluptuous body, which places her groin directly in front of my face, and offers me her hand. "Come on, let's get naughty everywhere in this suite. It's got, like, a hundred rooms. By the time we're done, you won't worry about which I prefer—you or your devices. You'll know the answer for sure."

"The answer will be me."

"You got it."

I stand up and look straight into her eyes. "You are my girlfriend, Rika. There's nothing fake about us."

She smiles and kisses me. "I knew that already, but I'm glad you said it."

And I let her lead me off to another room, then another, and another. We do everything two people can do together with only their bodies and various pieces of furniture. Rika and I don't need toys. She's the most inventive woman I've ever been with, and I discover I can be awfully inventive too when I have her body as my inspiration.

And yes, Rika shags my brains out.

It feels bloody incredible.

Chapter Fifteen

Rika

I spend the next several weeks watching Dane Dixon open up and bloom like a big, sexy flower. Maybe that's not the best metaphor, but the facts are irrefutable. Dane still gets stressed out sometimes, but he lets himself relax and enjoy life too. Every time we go out on a date, he smiles and tells jokes that make us both laugh.

Sure, we're doing this for publicity. And yeah, the occasional photo of us shows up on social media or in the society section of a newspaper. When someone on social media names him The Dirty Dixon, my boyfriend seems uncomfortable with the title, but he quickly decides to roll with it. Chance and Reese get mentions too, but only as The Dirty Dixon's brothers. Their names are rarely mentioned.

Dane and I might have told each other in words that we're a real couple now, but our actions speak everything we don't say about the depth of our feelings for each other. We hold hands in public and in private, like in the elevator that takes us up to his suite. And my uptight Brit now loves to make out with me in all three of the suite's elevators. He shocks me, however, when he seduces me in one of them. It's so hot and fun that I beg him to do that every time we go to his hotel.

And he always gives me what I want.

We haven't used his toys yet, not even as foreplay. I insist we don't, though he keeps suggesting we should, because I'm not sure if he's over his fear of me liking his devices better than I like his body. Maybe in another week, we can play with his toys.

About ten days after we first had sex, Dane and I are in his office taking a coffee break. Yes, Dane takes breaks now. But for us, a "coffee break" means I sit on his lap in his chair and we kiss. A lot. Dane also loves to tickle me in places where I had no idea I was ticklish, like behind my left ear and in the centers of both palms. He's blowing a raspberry against my throat, making loud giggles burst out of me, when Celeste Arnaud marches into the office.

Well, we had left the door open. Noah has gotten used to our antics, and Dane even tells jokes that make Noah laugh.

Celeste stops on the other side of the desk, plants a hand on her hip, and raises her brows at us. Her lips kick up in a self-satisfied smile.

Dane peels his lips away from my throat but keeps his arms around my waist so I can't get off his lap. Not that I want to.

"Good afternoon, Celeste," he says, sounding so cheerful that it seems to knock her off kilter for a second or two, based on the way her mouth falls open a touch. "What can we do for you today?"

Her surprise melts into a delighted little smile. "I knew you two would hit it off. Am I a matchmaker or what?"

"What are you talking about? Rika and I found each other on our own."

"But I hired her to be your personal assistant. I knew she'd be an excellent match for you professionally, and I hoped she might turn out to be your perfect match in love too."

Dane's expression goes blank as he stares at Celeste. After a moment, he grins. "You do have great taste, in everything. I suppose I shouldn't be surprised you picked the right woman for me even if you didn't set out to do that."

"A happy accident." Celeste winks. "Or was it?"

Did she seriously hire me because she thought Dane and I would make a good couple? No, even Celeste isn't that sneaky. We do have to give her credit, though, for bringing us into each other's lives.

Celeste sits down across the desk from us. "I'm glad to see you happy, Dane, but you need to prepare yourself for what's coming. The buildup to the re-launch kicks into high gear next week. That means public appearances—and I don't mean just having dinner with Rika at a fancy restaurant."

Dane groans and slumps in his chair, with me still on his lap.

At least Celeste and Reese took Dane's face off the packaging and changed the brand name so it no longer says "Dane's Delights" on the boxes. But I know Dane is not looking forward to press conferences or whatever it is Celeste and her marketing team have in mind.

"What do you want me to do?" Dane asks, sounding like he's about to be arrested instead of about to become filthy rich.

Celeste vowed she'd make him a billionaire, but twice he told me he's not sure he wants that.

"Haven't you checked your email?" Celeste asks. "Reese sent you an itinerary half an hour ago."

"Oh, I, uh—" Dane squirms like he's trying to sit up straighter, but my body is holding him down. "I've been…distracted."

Celeste glances at me. "I can see that."

Dane reaches around me to bring up his emails on the computer on his desk. He seems to be trying to print the one from Reese, but once again, the fact I'm on his lap is complicating the task.

I shoo his hand away from the keyboard. "Let me do that."

A few clicks later, the printer spits out the itinerary. I lean way over to grab the sheet out of the printer, then I hand it to him and loop my arms around his neck. Sure, this has become a business meeting, but I know Dane wants me to stay right where I am. He loves cuddling, especially when he's about to get news he won't like. I didn't mean to peek at the itinerary, but it was kind of inevitable. What? I had to look so I could make sure I printed out the right email.

Dane scans the list of events. He groans and shuts his eyes. "A fashion show? Why do I have to go to one of those? It's not like the models will be demonstrating my devices." His eyes fly wide. "Please tell me you're not having them do that."

Celeste laughs in her usual boisterous way. "Dane darling, you are so charmingly suspicious. No, your devices will not be featured at the fashion show. You will attend, with Rika, to show how hip and stylish you are." She eyes him with her analytical gaze. "I'd better send you over to Armani to get a decent suit. You can't show up to a fashion show wearing a suit from a discount store."

He glances down at his suit. "What's wrong this one? I got it at Marks & Spencer."

"Which is a department store in the UK." Celeste clucks her tongue while shaking her head. "Honestly, my dear, you need to dress that gorgeous body in the proper clothing. Rika will help you choose a suit. Won't you, darling?"

"Uh, sure," I say. I know nothing about designer duds, but what the heck, I'll give it a try. I think Dane looks hot in anything, so I may not be much help. In my opinion, though, he looks best in nothing at all.

We chat with Celeste for a few minutes, then she goes back to her office and Dane lets me drive the sports car he rented so I can get back to Eddie's house faster than the train can get me there. Eddie doesn't mind if I take a very long lunch once a week so I can hang out with Dane more. I make up the lost time by doing website maintenance for him on Saturday, from home. Eddie is one of the nicest people I've ever met, but Dane is my favorite person on earth.

Every weekend, we do something fun—like going to the zoo, which was Arden's suggestion, or visiting Chance and Elena in New Hampshire. Dane likes to sleep over at my apartment several times a week, and I think it's because he's used to a homey place instead of a luxury hotel suite. He grew up in a small town, after all. I'm from Chicago, but even I find that suite kind of off-putting. I mean, it's gorgeous and amazing, but it's not a home.

Our trip to the Armani store results in Dane buying three new suits and a tux. I buy a few dresses too. We both wince at the price tags—discreetly, so we won't offend the store employees—but Celeste insisted we should both have designer threads. She's paying for all of it, so we can't say no.

I have to admit Dane looks extra super yummy in an Armani suit. Am I drooling when I ogle him in that suit? Maybe. Who cares? My boyfriend is hot, hot, *hot.*

We survive the fashion show. I enjoy it, but Dane tolerates it. We get our picture taken by various members of the press, and the next day, we see ourselves in those ultra-chic clothes in various newspapers and magazines, plus some websites. More events follow, including a charity fundraising ball and a photo op at a store that's going to sell Dane's devices. It's a dizzying whirlwind of appearances that leaves us both exhausted.

One night, in Dane's opulent hotel suite, we reach another milestone. We've just made love, and the afterglow is pure bliss.

He turns onto his side and pulls me snug against him, our noses bumping. "I love you, Rika."

"I love you too, Dane."

A glow inside me suffuses my entire body. It's the glow of happiness, a kind I've never experienced before. I get the feeling he experiences the same thing, since his eyes have gone soft and warm, and he kisses me with a sweetness that triggers a dull but pleasant ache in my chest. Then he makes love to me again, infusing the act with all the emotions neither of us can fully express in words. I love this man, and he loves me. My crush has matured into the best thing that's ever happened to me.

The next morning, it's time for the hammer to drop.

It's re-launch day.

Chapter Sixteen

Dane

I stand on a temporary stage set up in the cavernous lobby at the global headquarters of Bonsoir Beauty Incorporated with a microphone on a stand positioned in front of me. Well, not me specifically. Not yet, anyway. Celeste will make her speech, then I will be required to speak. To a large audience. Full of reporters. With flash bulbs firing off like machine guns.

Bloody hell, it's hot in here. I'm starting to sweat, but when I glance around, no one else seems disturbed by the sweltering heat. Maybe it's just me. I don't want to do this.

Celeste begins her introduction, smiling and sounding as confident as ever. She gives a brief overview of Bonsoir and its subsidiaries, then she starts to talk about my corner of the Bonsoir domain. Any minute now she'll introduce me.

I resist the impulse to scratch under my shirt collar. Why do I feel like tiny insects are crawling all over my skin?

When I scan the crowd, I don't see anyone I recognize, so I turn to look at the people standing in the wings, behind a curtain. Reese is there. He gives me the thumbs-up sign and grins. Rika stands beside him. When she notices I'm looking at her, she smiles and mouths, "I love you."

I stand up straighter, lifting my chin. She loves me, and I won't let her down by stammering like an idiot in front of the international press.

"And now," Celeste says, spreading an arm toward me in a grand gesture, "may I introduce the genius behind our new line of sexual wellness devices—the gorgeous, charming, and talented Dane Dixon."

Christ, why did she have to give me an overblown introduction?

I glance at Rika again. This time she mouths, "You can do it."

So I do it. I walk up to the microphone and start my speech. Reese wrote it for me, but thankfully, he didn't include any racy jokes. What he wrote for me sounds like me, not like my little brother. I shouldn't be surprised. I've always known that Reese is cleverer than he used to let on and that he has a way with words. It's why he was successful as an advertising copywriter and why Celeste made him her vice president of advertising.

And I'm even more thankful that he kept the speech short.

"Thank you for coming today," I say, surprising myself with how composed I sound. "I'm proud to present our new line of sexual wellness devices for women—Bonsoir Delights, designed by me and manufactured by our extraordinary teams in the US, UK, Canada, the European Union, and a dozen other locations around the world. Soon, we'll be selling these devices everywhere from Boston to Beijing, and from Norway to New Zealand." I pause for a second, but not because I'm nervous. Not anymore. I'm following Reese's instructions in the script he gave me, which tell me to pause for dramatic effect. "Now, let me walk you through the products we have."

The rest of my speech goes by in a blur. I say all the words I'm meant to say, I hold up each device while I discuss it, and I don't stammer or choke on my own tongue. Not once. Not even when I have to say the name of the most embarrassingly titled device—the Jackrabbit. No, I am not going to explain why it's called that, not to this audience or to any of my friends or family, mostly because I have no idea. Reese came up with the name. He says his wife, Arden, gave him the idea. I don't want to know how or why she did that.

It's one of the two new devices I created. The second one won't be unveiled quite yet. I'm planning a private reveal for one person, the woman who inspired it. When I told Celeste I wanted to delay the announcement, she didn't complain. She said, "Yes, Dane darling, whatever my favorite employee wants."

"Shouldn't Reese be your favorite employee?" I'd asked. "He is your grandson-in-law."

"And I adore Reese, but I adore you even more." She patted my cheek. "Let's not tell Reese that. It's our little secret."

I've wrapped up my speech, so I walk behind the curtain. Celeste assured me I wouldn't need to answer questions from the press. She'll handle that. I hear her voice, projected by the speakers, as I pull Rika into my arms and hold her tight.

"So fucking glad that's over," I groan.

Reese chuckles. "You really aren't built for the public life, are you?"

"No, I'm not." I pull back enough to see Rika's face. Her smile is bright and loving. "Can we talk alone? I want to discuss something with you."

"Sure thing."

Reese winks at me. "Yes, Dane, you drag your girlfriend into a closet or whatever and have her shag you until you can't see straight. That'll make you feel much better."

"Piss off, Reese."

I don't drag Rika into a closet, but I do drag her out to the limousine Celeste hired to take us to and from the headquarters. We kiss for the entire ride back to my hotel, and that kissing involves plenty of groping as well as Rika's hand inside my trousers. I want to get my hand under her skirt, but it's the sort that's so bloody long and narrow that I can't get any part of me under it.

Once we get inside my suite, I strip off all her clothing and mine too, then I lay her down on the bed.

"I have a surprise for you," I say as I crawl up the bed to crouch over her beautiful body.

"You said you want to talk about something." She clasps her hands above her head, smiling in that subtle, sexy way I love. "But we're naked, so I'm thinking a conversation isn't tops on your list of things to do."

"We can talk after." I pull open the drawer in the bedside table and bring out a velvet bag. "Your surprise is in here. I made something just for you, because of you, and you're the first human on earth to see it. I made the prototype myself."

"Is this a new device?"

"Yes."

She cradles my face in her hands, the desire in her expression softened by a tenderness that always sets off a pang behind my ribs. "I told you before, I don't need your devices. I want you, Dane."

"But we can play with my devices. I know you'd like that." I tug the velvet bag open, reaching inside it. "I know you want me, without any mechanical aids, and I'm not worried about that anymore. But I want to play with you, Rika."

Her smile gets bigger, and her eyes sparkle. "I'd love that."

I knew she would, and I can't wait to do that. Pulling out the item I'd kept inside the velvet bag, I slip it onto my hand.

"That's a glove," she says, her forehead crinkling along with her brows. She's so fucking adorable when she's confused and aroused. "It looks soft, and I love that, but—"

"It is soft. It's made from the finest microfiber on earth." I spread my gloved hand over her belly and squeeze a tiny button on the inside of the glove's cuff. It begins to vibrate, not as much as other devices I've made, but with a gentle vibration meant to tease her. "How does this feel?"

She stiffens for a few seconds, then her entire body relaxes, and she hums with satisfaction. "That feels soooo good."

While I glide my gloved hand over her belly, I watch her enraptured expression, and blood starts to rush down to my cock. "I thought about making the glove from silk, but that would drive up the price. I want every woman to have the opportunity to feel the way you look right now. You're gorgeous, Rika, and I want to shag you until you're half out of your mind."

"Yes, please." She writhes and moans when I cup her breast with my gloved hand. "You really are a genius, Dane."

I flick my thumb over her nipple.

She jerks and cries out. "Oh God, do that again."

"Like it, do you?" I flick my thumb again, then brush my fingers over her areola in slow circles. Her throaty moan makes my cock twitch. "Time to come for me, love."

I drag my hand down her belly, pausing over her mound only long enough to make her squirm and gasp, then I push my hand between her folds. Naturally, I made the ultra-soft material waterproof. When I whisk my finger around her clit, she goes off.

"Dane!" she shouts while her body goes rigid and her fingers clench the sheets.

Once I've made her come for as long as she can stand to, I turn off the glove and toss it onto the table.

And I make love to her for an hour.

While we enjoy the afterglow, we talk about the future.

"This isn't the life I want," I tell her. "I thought I did, but I don't. I'm not meant for a public life."

"Yeah, I figured. You were amazing at the press conference, but I know you don't like doing that kind of thing."

"Would it, uh, disappoint you if I, um, sort of…quit my job?"

She kisses me. "I want you to be happy. Quit, if that's what you need to do."

"I'd much rather go home to England and start designing different kinds of devices. No more vibrators. Maybe I can help people with physical therapy or something. Haven't decided yet."

"Whatever you decide to do, I know you'll be a genius at it." She dances her fingertips over my chest. "And I'll go anywhere with you. England, the South Pole, wherever. Besides, England is a lot closer to where my parents live in Sweden."

God, I love her.

The next day, we break the news to Celeste. She's not upset about it. In fact, she doesn't even seem surprised—and she offers me a severance package so generous that I can take my time figuring out what the next phase of my life looks like. Our life. Rika and I will do this together, whatever "this" turns out to be.

A few days later, Chance and Elena pick us up at the airport in the jet they chartered, and we all fly to England. When we get to my parents' house, everyone is there, including Reese and Arden as well as Arden's parents, Elena's brother, and Rika's parents. I had them flown in from Sweden since I know Rika hasn't seen them in quite some time.

One of the guests has stayed at the periphery, glancing around like he's uncomfortable.

"Who's that guy?" Rika asks.

"That's my cousin, Grey. He's a bit shy around strangers, and this is the first time he's met you, Arden, and Elena."

"Couldn't his parents make it? You invited everyone else."

"I let Chance and Elena do the inviting." I slip my arm around her waist. "But Grey never knew his mother, and his father died several years ago. We're all the family he has."

"That's so sad. We should adopt him. Not literally, of course."

"Let's talk about that later." I move in front of her and drop to one knee, pulling out a small box and flipping its lid up. "Fredrika Maria Solberg, I love you more than anything or anyone in the entire universe. You changed my life and showed me everything I'd been missing. I owe you my happiness, a debt I want to spend the rest of my life repaying. Will you marry me?"

She bursts into tears. "Yes, Dane, of course I will. I love you so much."

I slide the ring onto her finger.

Reese whoops. Chance whistles. Their wives shriek and jump up and down. Rika's mother cries while her husband grins. Kyle Linwood pumps his fists in the air and grunts like a gorilla or…something. My mother and father rush up to us to hug me, then Rika, then me again. My mother is crying too.

Grey shuffles up to us after everyone else has gone off to arrange some sort of celebration that I'm sure will be embarrassing. My cousin shakes my hand and kisses Rika's cheek. "Congratulations. And welcome to the family, Rika."

"Thank you." She kisses his cheek. "I hope we'll get to know each other a lot better."

"I'd like that."

My fiancée wants to take Grey under her wing. I love that she cares so much about a man she's just met, simply because he's my cousin. Rika is wonderful in every way.

A few more people arrive for the party, but most of them are mates of Reese and Chance. I don't have any close friends, but I plan to change that.

Rika sidles up to me and whispers, "Who's the hottie talking to Chance? Another cousin?"

"No, that's Richard Hunter. He and Chance have known each other since university. Richard owns a publishing company that he inherited from his father."

"Hmm. Is he a nice guy?"

"Seems to be, yes."

"Is he married? Or does he have a girlfriend?"

"Not that I know of."

She lifts onto her tiptoes to peer across the room at Richard. "You know my sister, Maddie, is coming to visit us next week. And she's single too."

"No meddling, Rika."

She bats her eyelashes at me with fake innocence. "All I want to do is introduce them."

I don't get the chance to order her not to meddle, because Reese approaches me. Rika leaves us alone while she wanders over to Richard.

Reese grins and slaps me on the shoulder. "Told you, mate. I said you'd be next, and here you are volunteering for the ball and chain."

Being chained to Rika doesn't sound like torture. I never want to let her go, so if a wedding ring shackles me to her, I absolutely do volunteer for it.

"That's right," I tell Reese. "I'm signing up for that ball and chain, as long as it's attached to Rika for the rest of our lives."

And if my fiancée has her way, Richard Hunter will be next.

Love the

Hot Brits

series?

Visit
AnnaDurand.com

to subscribe to her newsletter
for updates on forthcoming books in this series
&
to receive a free gift for signing up!

Anna Durand is a bestselling, multi-award-winning author of contemporary and paranormal romance. Her books have earned bestseller status on every major retailer and wonderful reviews from readers around the world. But that's the boring spiel. Here are the really cool things you want to know about Anna!

Born on Lachland Air Force Base in Texas, Anna grew up moving here, there, and everywhere thanks to her dad's job as an instructor pilot. She's lived in Texas (twice), Mississippi, California (twice), Michigan (twice), and Alaska—and now Ohio.

As for her writing, Anna has always made up stories in her head, but she didn't write them down until her teen years. Those first awful books went into the trash can a few years later, though she learned a lot from those stories. Eventually, she would pen her first romance novel, the paranormal romance *Willpower*, and she's never looked back since.

Want even more details about Anna? Get access to her extended bio when you subscribe to her newsletter and download the free bonus ebook, *Hot Scots Confidential*. You'll also get hot deleted scenes, character interviews, fun facts, and more! Plus you'll receive the short story *Tempted by a Kiss*, two bonus chapters for *One Hot Chance*, and a bonus audiobook chapter narrated for you by Shane East.

Visit AnnaDurand.com to sign up.